Lockdown Board Meetings 2020

Martin Hesketh

Copyright © 2012 R M Hesketh

All rights reserved.

ISBN: **9798644710126**

DEDICATION

To all the Stakeholders from the Lockdown Board Meetings Community who took the time to respond to the ramblings every day and shared a crispy dry one

CONTENTS

	Acknowledgments	I
1	Lockdown Begins	1
2	Ada Acts Up	3
3	Ada Smells Pleasant	6
4	The Toilet Roll Incident	9
5	Ada Found Guilty	12
6	The Kitchen Door	15
7	The Weather Gets Better	18
8	The Big Foreign Bird	21
9	Horny Frank's Valuable Lesson	24
10	The Interview	27
11	Rosie Pays a Visit	30
12	Beardy's Misunderstanding	33
13	Beardy is Bang On	36
14	Her Indoors Blocks the Kitchen Door	40
15	Dr Beardy's Noo-Noo Prognosis	43
16	Crispy Dry Time is a Thing	46
17	Karen the Sheep Shows Up	50
18	Karen the Sheep is in Hiding	53
19	Their Little Hearts are Bursting	56
20	Ada's in Big Trouble	59

21	Ada Gets Locked Up	63
22	Her Indoors Favours Horny Frank	66
23	It's Rabbit Day	70
24	Spencer's Inflexibility Issue	73
25	RLT Uprising	76
26	RLT Attack	79
27	Bigger Flap Required	82
28	Plan B	85
29	Foxy the Foxy Nosed Fox	88
30	Karen gets Snarly	92
31	The Snickerdoodles	95
32	The Pecker Kids Go Missing	98
33	The Passport	101
34	The Return of the Big Foreign Bird	105
35	Tucker the Sheepdog	108
36	The Death of the Blue Furry Creature	112
37	The Hostage Exchange	115
38	The Farm	118
39	The Black Cat	121
40	Regan from the Special Branch	124
41	Her Nextdoor and Lulu	127
42	The Camp Follower Policy	130
43	Ultrasound Frequencies	133

44	The Treasure	136
45	Downtown Boy	139
46	The Council of Five	142
47	Paradise	146
48	Loko Foko	149
49	Special Unit for Foreign Affairs	153
50	The Backslider	157
51	Ada Goes Missing	161
52	A New Stink	164
53	Sandy Cheeks	168
54	Robins Cider	172
55	Spud's Eyeballing Event	176
56	East of The Farm	180
57	Mike with a Y	183
58	The Baby Sheep	187
59	The Hard Border Goes Up	190
60	The Flag of Liberty	193

ACKNOWLEDGMENTS

To say I wrote a book underestimates what it really takes to write a book, so I do apologise to all proper writers. All I did was cut and paste my community page ramblings, into a book format. I would never have dreamt of putting this book together if it wasn't for the members of the, 'I grew up in Belfast and am proud of it' community page, the members, of the 'Chelsham, Farleigh, Warlingham' community page, and of course my friends and members of the 'Lockdown Board Meetings 2020' community page. It was their suggestion that I should write a book as a keepsake to remind them of their coffee mornings and crispy dry afternoons as they read my mad ramblings during the lockdown event. I would also like to thank Her Indoors for putting up with my crispy dry times while she was battling on the NHS front line and still managed to smile as we compared our day's events. I would also like to say a special thank you to Anya for proofreading this collection of ramblings, which I can tell you was no easy task.

1. LOCKDOWN BEGINS

1st Lockdown Board Meeting: Sat, 21st March 2020

In Attendance:

Me (Chair)

Spud II (Head of cat dept)

Spencer (Head of bigger dog dept)

Ada (Head of smaller dog dept)

Horny Frank (Head of horny rabbit dept)

Beardy (Head of not so horny rabbit dept)

Apologies - None

Call to order 08:00hrs

1. There were sufficient members for a quorum
2. No previous minutes for approval

3. Statement from the Chair: Boris stated that a New Battle of Britain has begun, so that's not so good. Boris closes all pubs and restaurants, so that's not good either. Boris vows to pay their wages, so that's good.
4. Business updates:
    4.1 Spud: Spud was concerned about food. The Chair assured Spud that Pets at Home was still open, there were no queues and shelves were still full of Felix Pouches. Spud asked would the Chair be going today to get more. The Chair stated that we had plenty, so there was no need. Spud asked the Chair to define *plenty*. The Chair stated two months' worth. Spud suggest a year's worth might be more appropriate. The Chair asked if this issue could be parked for the moment and maybe take it up later offline.
    4.2 Spencer: Spencer asked if walks were still available during lockdown. The Chair stated that they were. He asked if there were any new protocols/policies regarding sniffing arses and licking pee-pee sticks. The Chair stated that as long as the sniffing and licking practices were kept between dogs that would be fine, as humans are isolating against everything, especially the licking of pee-pee sticks, and especially in public.
    4.3 Ada: Ada reminded Spencer and the Chair that bitches have lickable parts as well and was curious to know as to why this aspect was omitted. The Chair assured Ada that it was just a slip of the tongue. Ada suggested that if food becomes short, would it be appropriate to eat the rabbits first? The Chair assured Ada that it would absolutely never probably get that bad.
    4.4 Horny Frank: Horny Frank suggested that if it did get that bad, Beardy would make for a better stew than him, Beardy's fatter and has lots of protein in him at the moment.
    4.5 Beardy: Beardy added that he hates being locked up and infringed upon every day and that he would gladly offer himself up to be eaten should the need arise. The Chair thanked Beardy for volunteering.
5. Other business – None

2. ADA PLAYS UP

2nd Lockdown Board Meeting: Sun, 22nd March 2020

In Attendance:

Me (Chair)

Spud II (Head of cat dept)

Spencer (Head of bigger dog dept)

Ada (Head of smaller dog dept, Acting Head of not so horny rabbit dept)

Horny Frank (Head of horny rabbit dept)

Beardy (Head of not so horny rabbit dept)

Apologies - None

Call to order 08:00hrs

1. There were sufficient members for a quorum
2. Minutes of previous meeting approved

3. Statement from the Chair: The virus hits Italy hard, so that's not so good. A curfew starts in India, so that's interesting. Beach parties continue in Miami, so that's interesting too.
4. Business updates:
    4.1 Ada: Ada stated that she is currently looking after the 'not so horny rabbit department' in Beardy's absence. Ada added that Beardy is now isolating as he was having fluctuating temperatures between 40°C and 40.1°C and had a wet nose, so he's staying in his hutch.
    4.2 Horny Frank: Horny Frank raised concerns that a dog is acting up as Head of a rabbit department. Ada stated that she was not actually acting up but merely helping out temporarily. Horny Frank stated that the issue was her being a *dog*, and that her skill set was somewhat questionable, and was concerned that she wouldn't be able to fulfil the full range of duties as she's anatomically somewhat different. Horny Frank also asked would Ada be taking up space in the hutch while carrying out her new temporary duties. The Chair stated that Ada would not be placed in the hutch at this moment in time. Ada suggested that Horny Frank was being racist and most likely a Nazi.
    4.3 Spencer: Spencer stated that he was concerned about the current lack of doo-doo bags and that the picking up of doo-doo during walks was at best sparse. Spencer reminded the Chair that neither he nor Ada were police dogs or sheepdogs on duty, so therefore, there's a legal requirement for their doo-doo to be picked up. The Chair stated that there is currently a shortage of doo-doo bags due to people panic buying, but the Chair has been reassured by Pets at Home, that they are restocking the shelves quickly and restricting customers to only one box of doo-doo bags per family. Spencer also suggested that if Beardy was ill, he should get less food rations. Ada strongly argued that on the contrary, we should be feeding him up just in case we need that stew.
    4.4 Ada: Ada had nothing further to add.
    4.5 Spud: Spud asked if these emergency board meetings are going to be a daily occurrence could the time be changed, as he only gets in at 08:00hrs and is pretty much cattle trucked. He also asked was it still ok for him to do his doo-doo outside without having it picked up? The Chair states that it's only dogs that aren't allowed to do their doo-doo outside without having it picked up. Ada asked, with her rabbit hat on, could she now do her doo-doo outside without having it picked up?

The Chair stated that even when she's carrying out her rabbit duties, she is still a dog, and therefore has to comply with dog rules until further notice.
5. Other business – None

3. ADA SMELLS PLEASANT

3rd Lockdown Board Meeting: Mon, 23rd March 2020

In Attendance:

Me (Chair)

Spud II (Head of cat dept)

Spencer (Head of bigger dog dept)

Ada (Head of smaller dog dept)

Horny Frank (Head of horny rabbit dept)

Beardy (Head of not so horny rabbit dept)

Apologies - None

Call to order 15:00hrs

1. There were sufficient members for a quorum
2. Minutes of previous meeting approved

3. Statement from the Chair: Boris wants to introduce Italian type restrictions to enforce social distancing, so that's interesting. Boris stated that if the rules aren't obeyed, a stricter lockdown will be put in place, so that's not so good.
4. Business updates:
    4.1 Beardy: Beardy stated that he's happy to be back and it was a false alarm, he had not contracted this new human flu but still had some of the symptoms and will continue to self-monitor. Beardy also stated that he couldn't get through to 111 as he didn't have a phone and was concerned about putting on weight during the lockdown. Ada added that Beardy was looking great and suggested low fat honey nut loops with a sprinkling of sugar, before each meal.
    4.2 Horny Frank: Horny Frank asked if the new human flu could be sexually transmitted and should he start considering rubbers? The Chair stated that the question of whether the new human flu is sexually transmitted is largely irrelevant to the risks of having sex with an infected animal. The bug that causes this new human flu is transmitted through secretions from the mouth and nose, even if you don't kiss the one you're having sex with, you're likely to be touching each other's surfaces with soiled paws. Horny Frank asked for a definitive yes or no to the rubber question. The Chair stated no, and not even sure Pets at Home sell rubbers for rabbits but will check and report back.
    4.3 Spud: Spud stated that he was pleased with the new time slot at 15:00hrs. He also stated that when he was out and about last night, he was concerned there was still a lot of activity and that not all animals were taking this lockdown seriously enough. It was a lovely night, and they were all over the place despite social distancing advice following the escalation of the new human flu. It is just socially irresponsible, and he bets it'll be no different tonight. Obviously, he had to be out and about to get food, and anyway, he's been identified as a Key cat, a front-line cat if you like.
    4.4 Spencer: Spencer stated that now Ada was coming of age and is starting to smell quite pleasant, should we be considering more physical distancing between the big dog department and the small dog department while in lockdown? Ada stated that Spencer can foxtrot right off, and if he sticks his lipstick in my face once more, she'll bite the scrawny thing off. The Chair stated that these are very trying times and we must be more

considerate with one another but will check *gov.uk* to see if there's any advice regarding dogs in heat and report back.
4.5 Ada had nothing more to add.
5. Other business – None

4. THE TOILET ROLL INCIDENT

4th Lockdown Board Meeting: Tues, 24th March 2020

In Attendance:

Me (Chair)

Spud II (Head of cat dept)

Spencer (Head of bigger dog dept)

Ada (Head of smaller dog dept)

Horny Frank (Head of horny rabbit dept)

Beardy (Head of not so horny rabbit dept)

Apologies - None

Call to order 15:00hrs

1. There were sufficient members for a quorum
2. Minutes of previous meeting approved

3. Statement from the Chair: Boris stated that - you must stay at home, this is a national emergency, so that's not good. Boris also stated that 'many more will die', so that's definitely not good.
4. Business from last meeting:
   4.1 The Chair stated that he checked with Pets at Home, and they do not sell rubbers for rabbits, nor do they know anywhere that does.
   4.2 The Chair also stated that he checked the *gov.uk* website regarding dogs in heat and physical distancing, and as informative as the site is, couldn't see anything on dogs at all.
5. Proposed topic: The Chair is allowing a non-agenda item to be discussed instead of business, and that today's business will be added to tomorrow's business tomorrow.
   5.1 The Damaged Toilet Roll Incident. The Chair was very concerned that the last roll of toilet paper has been damaged to the extent that it has now been deemed unusable. The damaged toilet paper was discovered late yesterday afternoon in the kitchen area when the Chair arrived back at the house. The Chair appreciates that lockdowns can be tedious, and mischief/accidents can occur, but as this was the last toilet roll in the house and there's no more in the shops, this calls for a more severe punishment than the normal boot in the hole. As all members of the Board were present in the house at the time, except the Chair, he would like the culprit to own up and save mass hole bootings with extras.
   5.2 Horny Frank stated that he was in the front room resting most of the time, but could hear a commotion coming from the kitchen area. Plus, there's photographic evidence of the culprit with the toilet paper in *her* possession, what more do you need? He also stated that he was sure mass bootings with extras wouldn't be required.
   5.3 Ada stated that she was sound asleep, then woke up, and there was toilet paper all over the show, and yes, she touched it to see what it was, but surely that doesn't warrant a boot in the hole with or without extras. Plus, Ada added, that she's not at all happy with the photographs that accompany the minutes, who even does that? It's clearly biased, and she will be seeking official guidance.
   5.4 Spud stated that he was out for his early afternoon hunt and got back shortly after lunch. Ada was alone in the kitchen asleep but woke up slightly as he came through the cat flap. He added that there was no toilet paper there then. However, he stated that later on there was a lot of noise, which of course

usually occurs when the Chair leaves the house, the place turns into Toy Story 6. Spud also asked what the *extras* were going to be, which is to accompany the boot in the hole? The Chair said that he had not decided on the extras yet, but will inform the Board in due course.

5.5 Spencer stated that he was mostly patrolling the house, which he says is one of his main duties as Head of bigger dog department, especially during these stressful and troubling times, somebody has to take the initiative, all this wandering around obviously with no idea what two metres is! He happened to be upstairs checking out one of the bedrooms when he heard lots of running around, almost like hopping around sounds. When he got back to his bed in the kitchen area, there was toilet paper all over the show. He also added that although he is pictured in close vicinity of the toilet paper, he can assure the Board that he didn't touch it.

5.6 Beardy stated that he was mostly in the conservatory area but did have spurts of hopping occasionally, can't help the hopping, the hopping just happens, he hears a noise and the legs just straighten out and up he goes! Although he didn't spend much time in the kitchen area when the hopping was happening, he once or twice ended up near the kitchen area, and he did see Ada with a mouth full of toilet paper!

5.7 The Chair stated that he was disappointed that the culprit hadn't come forward, but he did have enough evidence to solve the case. He will go through all of the evidence again tonight, take some legal advice if required, and make a statement at tomorrow's Board meeting tomorrow, before business updates resume.

6. Other business – None

5. ADA FOUND GUILTY

5th Lockdown Board Meeting, Wed, 25th March 2020

In Attendance:

Me (Chair)

Spud II (Head of cat dept)

Spencer (Head of bigger dog dept)

Ada (Head of smaller dog dept)

Horny Frank (Head of horny rabbit dept)

Beardy (Head of not so horny rabbit dept)

Apologies - None

Call to order 15:00hrs

1. There were sufficient members for a quorum
2. Minutes of previous meeting approved

3. Statement from the Chair: Boris wants volunteers to bolster the NHS, so that's not so good. Boris's mate Matt wants Fit Brits to sign up to a national service of volunteers to help deliver stuff, so that's interesting. Military logistic vehicles spotted on Westminster Bridge delivering face masks to St Thomas' hospital, so that's handy.
4. Business from last meeting: The Chair's announcement: following on from yesterday's incident regarding the damaged last toilet roll. I have gone through all the evidence from yesterday's statements and concluded that there is no doubt in my mind, that Ada damaged the last toilet roll. She damaged it on her own and with full intent. I have no choice but to prosecute her to the fullest extent of the Law. She will receive a boot in the hole at a predetermined time in the future, and as extra punishments, she will not be able to come into the front room for her usual cuddles for two consecutive nights starting with immediate effect. Ada's announcement: you are having a laugh, this is a complete setup, and what's this about a boot in the hole in the future, I'm going to receive a boot in hole sometime in the future? I won't even know what it's for! I'll become a nervous wreck, and end up a troubled dog; I'll then probably bite some nasty kid and get locked up in Battersea Dogs Home with all the other losers, and lose all my cuteness.
5. Business Updates:
   5.1 Horny Frank: Horny Frank stated that he was glad this horrible business was over us now.
   5.2 Spencer: Spencer stated that as we were back to business as usual and with the new lockdown conditions coming from Boris, he'd be stepping up his patrols during the day, he will start at night as well. He added that he now has the authority to stop and question anybody that looks somewhat dodgy. As he was now beginning to patrol in the evening, he asked, could the kitchen door be left open? The Chair stated no.
   5.3 Spud: Spud stated that he had no current business to report and that the new lockdown requirements don't apply to him as he was a front-line Key cat. He also stated, referring to the Chair's punishment statement, that not getting cuddles, is hardly a punishment, and maybe should consider two boots in the hole, one now and one at a later date when Ada isn't expecting it. The Chair stated that he was sticking with the original punishment plans.
   5.4 Beardy: Beardy asked if Spencer would stop relieving himself up against the rabbit hutch, it seems to be every day now and it stinks! Horny Frank thanked Beardy for bringing that up

and added that as the Spring is here, he noticed that the hutch door is left open at night but expressed concerns that it's still very cold at night. Beardy said that he didn't mind the door being opened at night as he likes to take a hop out into the run area and annoy the fox types. Horny Frank suggested that nevertheless, they should try and keep warmer at night and that their spooning was cosy and warm and that they should do more of it. Beardy added, perhaps, but it's never only just spooning though is it? Everybody enjoys a wee spoon now and again, especially when it's a bit chilly, but Horny Frank takes spooning to a whole new level! The Chair stated that it is getting warmer, and the hutch door stays open. It's too much of a hassle going out every night to close it, especially when it's still so cold outside. The Chair concluded that pissing on the hutch is now a bootable offence if caught in the act.

6. Other business – The Chair announced that some of our Stakeholders have complained about the Lockdown Board Meeting times. It was remarked that the minutes are published eight hours before the actual time the meeting takes place, and this confuses some of them. Therefore, we will be bringing forward the meetings to before the time the minutes are published. Thus, the new time is 06:00hrs.

6. THE KITCHEN DOOR

6th Lockdown Board Meeting: Thurs, 26th March 2020

In Attendance:

Me (Chair)

Spud II (Head of cat dept)

Spencer (Head of bigger dog dept)

Ada (Head of smaller dog dept)

Horny Frank (Head of horny rabbit dept)

Beardy (Head of not so horny rabbit dept)

Apologies - None

Call to order 06:00hrs

1. There were sufficient members for a quorum
2. Minutes of previous meeting approved

3. Business from last meeting: None
4. Statement from the Chair: Police are using drones to watch walkers heading to beauty spots, so that's not good. Twitchers who flocked to see a rare bird in Gloucestershire have been sent home, so that's funny. Children are sending pictures to isolated older folk, so that's nice. Boris stated that he would pay 80% of struggling business's wages, so that's good.
5. Business Updates:
    5.1 Spencer: Spencer stated that he was very sorry, but he peed in the kitchen area, in fact up against the fridge. It wasn't a full blast but merely a little spurt. He added that he was extremely embarrassed and will endeavour never to let it happen again. Spud expressed some concern. He asked if it could be the heat thing with the bitch. Ada reminded Spud that she was sitting right there, and she does have a name! Spud was also concerned that Ada wasn't 'done' yet. The Chair stated that Ada would be spayed soon, he added that he wasn't sure if the vets were opened but will check and report back.
    5.2 Ada: Ada wanted to know why her? Why is it that she has to go under the knife? Why not cut Spencer's bits off instead? Surely the problem lies with Spencer not controlling his spurts! Is this because of the bloody toilet rolls again! The Chair assured Ada that it had nothing to do with the toilet rolls, but she can't go around arousing Spencer willy-nilly like.
    5.3 Spud: Spud stated that he didn't seem to have that type of problem and in fact, he never had a lipstick problem either. Are cats different in some way? asked Spud. The Chair stated that Spud was castrated when he was a little kitten. Spud asserted that he was utterly shocked and wanted to know where his choice was in the matter? The Chair stated that Spud didn't have a choice in the matter and that castrating cats was a rule of thumb. Spud insisted on a reason. The Chair stated that it makes Spud less likely to fight other cats, less likely to roam and go missing, less likely to get hit by a car or get cat AIDS.
    5.4 Beardy: Beardy asked if Spencer could patrol the garden area more. With everybody staying indoors nowadays, the foxy foxes are getting braver! One came into the garden yesterday, with its wee foxy eyes and its wee foxy ears, poking its wee foxy nose where it didn't belong. The Chair assured Beardy that the hutch is entirely foxy proof.
    5.5 Horny Frank: Horny Frank agreed with Beardy. These foxy foxes are becoming more and more of an issue and that extra

garden security would be very much appreciated by both rabbit departments. Spencer agreed with the extra patrolling and therefore asked the Chair if the kitchen door could be left open all day. The Chair disagreed and added that the kitchen door will only be opened as and when required. Ada stated that she would patrol during the day as she can get through the cat flap. Spencer was concerned that Ada didn't have the training. Ada wanted to know what training you need to bite the hole of a mangy fox. Spencer argued that unwelcomed visitor control was a serious matter. Ada reminded Spencer that pissing all over the fridge in the kitchen area is a serious matter and if she ends up getting her noo-noo chopped up, she's coming after his sweetbreads.

6. Other business – None

7. THE WEATHER GETS BETTER

7th Lockdown Board Meeting: Fri, 27th March 2020

In Attendance:

Me (Chair)

Spud II (Head of cat dept)

Spencer (Head of bigger dog dept)

Ada (Head of smaller dog dept)

Horny Frank (Head of horny rabbit dept)

Beardy (Head of not so horny rabbit dept)

Apologies - None

Call to order 06:00hrs

1. There were sufficient members for a quorum
2. Minutes of previous meeting approved

3. Statement from the Chair: Hospitals brace for a virus Tsunami, so that's not so good. NHS staff and care workers are applauded, so that's good. The housing market has plunged into chaos, so that's not so good either.
4. Business from last meeting: The Chair stated that the vets are still open.
5. Business Updates:
    5.1 Ada: Ada noted that the Chair, and the other humans are now starting to cook and eat outside in the garden area and wondered had there been a change in the restrictions. The Chair stated that as the weather is getting better, and as we approach the summer, more eating and cooking will take place outside. Spud stated that he didn't think much of it to begin with but realised that the cooking method itself was in fact, cooking meat over smoking coals. Aren't there restrictions on meat? asked Spud. After all added Ada, we're subjected to Lily's Kitchen Chicken Casserole, and the chicken content is at best questionable. The Chair is cooking real delicious chicken right in front of us; she can't even have a conversation without choking on her own slobber! Thought pasta and rice was the only food allowed? argued Ada. The Chair replied that no meat restrictions are currently in place, and pasta and rice were actually very hard to get now.
    5.2 Spud: Spud stated that as much as he agreed with Ada's concerns about the blatant cooking and eating of meat outside in the garden area, he doesn't mind Lily's Kitchen Chicken Casserole, especially with a handful of Whiskas Complete Dry over the top, yum yum.
    5.3 Horny Frank: Horny Frank stated as we're on the subject of food, he noticed another new development. Just as the grass is starting to grow, and lovely it is too, the Chair is cutting it! Like what's that all about? The hay is ok, he doesn't care about chicken meat, but fresh grass, come on! The smell alone is driving him and Beardy nuts. Move the hutch around for God's sake; they'll cut the grass for the Chair. The Chair stated that the hutch is moved twice weekly during the cleaning process. The timing of this process is determined by the amount of poop there is. So, replied Horny Frank, if there's more poop, there's more grass - *poop for grass*.
    5.4 Beardy: Beardy thanked Spencer for guarding the garden area and Ada for her support. No foxes entered the garden area during the day. However, they are still around at night and wondered why Ada wasn't patrolling more at night? Ada

stated that she didn't patrol all night because she was asleep some of it. Currently, she added, the Dog Security Branch working in cooperation with both dog departments is hindered by the current kitchen door policy. If the kitchen door policy was relaxed, then the Dog Security Branch could devise an on-call rota that would meet the requirements of both rabbit departments. The Chair commented that he had taken these concerns on board, and although parked, will consider them for discussion at a later date should the situation worsen. However, for now, the current kitchen door policy is still in place.

6. Other business – The Chair thanked the members for clapping their paws last night for our wonderful NHS.

8. THE BIG FOREIGN BIRD

8th Lockdown Board Meeting: Sat, 28th March 2020

In Attendance:

Me (Chair)

Spud II (Head of cat dept)

Spencer (Head of bigger dog dept)

Ada (Head of smaller dog dept)

Horny Frank (Head of horny rabbit dept)

Beardy (Head of not so horny rabbit dept)

Apologies - None

Call to order 06:00hrs

1. There were sufficient members for a quorum
2. Minutes of previous meeting approved

Lockdown Board Meetings 2020

3. Business from last meeting: none
4. Statement from the Chair: Boris is infected, so that's not good. Boris's mates Matt and Prof Chris are infected too, so that's not good either. The Daily Star's solution is - scrub your knobs and knockers, so that's informative. Mr T has a drug to sort the virus and stated that it'd be all done and dusted by Easter, so that's good. As Mr T is mates with Boris, he will give him some of the new drug too, so that's great.
5. End of Week Statement from the Chair: We have been in *lockdown* for a week now. I want to thank all the departments for their cooperation during these stressful times, and glad our Stakeholders are very happy with our updates. From what I gather, the situation with the new human flu grows worse, and it's quite possible that further restrictions could be enforced. However, the daily lockdown board meetings will continue until further notice.
6. Business Updates:
    6.1 Beardy: Beardy asked, had any rabbits died of the new human flu yet? The Chair stated that according to the World Health Organisation, there is no evidence of cats, dogs or even rabbits, getting the new human flu and that there's no justification for taking measures against animals. Beardy stated that he heard from Karen that it's worse than the myxomatosis flu, and already six billion rabbits have died in Iran, and the Government is keeping it under wraps. Ada argued, look bright eyes, only the humans get it, and stop listening to Karen, whoever she is, she doesn't know diddly squat. The Chair assured Beardy that he gets all the up to date communications from around the World, and there's no mention of rabbits anywhere. Beardy stated that that's his point exactly.
    6.2 Horny Frank: Horny Frank reiterated Beardy's concern and asked that the Chair notifies the Board when 'no justification for measures' becomes 'justification for measures.' The Chair assured Horny Frank that 'justification for measures' will never happen. Horny Frank argued that, remember when that CJD flu was killing all the humans, who did they blame in the end, the poor cows. The cows were probably having their own Board meetings, being told- don't worry about any justification for measures, it'll never happen, then wallop…it's the cows they said, let's get them. Yeah tell it to the cows, they were so mad.
    6.3 Ada: Ada added that while everybody else was inside yesterday afternoon, a Big Foreign Bird entered the garden area. Not a

local avian, not even sure it was an avian, she added, never seen the like before. She stated that she chased it off using her super jumping powers and just missed it by a whisker. Can't be too careful nowadays, that avian flu stuff can be deadly also. Ask the chickens about their justification for measures!

6.4 Spud: Spud stated that this situation with the Big Foreign Bird was a one-off. He controls the avians. Ada's jumping powers are nothing compared to his, and that she should leave all the jumping stuff to him. That's why the local avians stay high up in the trees, Spud continued, any lower then wallop, game over. Beardy stated that he in fact, had seen the Big Foreign Bird as well, and it definitely isn't a local avian, probably comes from up Town. Anyway, it just drops in, grabs a snail then wings it. Ada argued that her jumping powers were well documented, and she will continue to jump as and when required.

6.5 Spencer: Spencer stated that he thinks the Big Foreign Bird came from up Town via the railway verge area, beyond the garden area. He reassured the Board that he patrols the railway verge area just near the perimeter of the garden area. He stated that he hadn't actually seen the Big Foreign Bird but will monitor the situation closely and introduce a daily sit rep until the crisis has been resolved. He suggested that we should consider closing the perimeter area between the garden area and the railway verge area. He will also instruct Ada to patrol further into the railway verge area. Spud argues that the avians, including the Big Foreign Bird, are his responsibility and he will join in on Spencer's daily sit rep too. The Chair stated that he would consider the closing of the perimeter between the garden area and the railway verge area in light of the recent development.

7. Other business – None

9. HORNY FRANK'S VALUABLE LESSON

9th Lockdown Board Meeting: Sun, 29th March 2020

In Attendance:

Me (Chair)

Spud II (Head of cat dept)

Spencer (Head of bigger dog dept)

Ada (Head of smaller dog dept)

Horny Frank (Head of horny rabbit dept)

Beardy (Head of not so horny rabbit dept)

Apologies - None

Call to order 07:00hrs

1. There were sufficient members for a quorum
2. Minutes of previous meeting approved

3. Business from last meeting: The Chair stated that the perimeter area between the garden area and the railway verge area would not be closed at this stage.
4. Statement from the Chair: The Government says - stay at home and stay two meters away from people if you go out, so that's interesting. Boris stated that - it's not such a difficult thing, just do it, so that's good. The BBC stated that two meters is equal to a bed, so that's handy.
5. Announcement from the Chair: I have three points to make. First of all, it's not 6 o'clock; it's 7 o'clock. There's been a time change, forgot to tell you yesterday, sorry about that and don't ask why, it's a long story, so adjust whatever you have to adjust to compensate, you might find feeding times somewhat odd, but tomorrow the meetings are back to 6 o'clock again, it might feel a bit early, but roll with it. Secondly, on Tuesday morning, I will not be available to Chair the lockdown board meeting. We currently have a tax issue- the Paying In department of the tax office claim that we owe them money. However, the Paying Out department of the tax office owes us money and a lot more than we owe the Paying In department. Now the Paying Out department is delaying payments because of the human flu, but for some reason, the Paying In department don't seem to have that same problem. Cut a long story short; I'm heading to up Town to sort it out. Therefore, I will need someone to act up as Chair for the Board meeting on Tuesday morning. I will postpone business updates on Monday morning to listen to anybody who wishes to apply for this prestigious acting-up position. Thirdly, Rosie, the white rabbit will be staying with us for a couple of days, and a temporary hutch will be erected to accommodate this visit.
6. New Joint Daily Situation Report: Spencer stated that the avians still keep their distance and no sign of the Big Foreign Bird or any other visitor types. Spud insists that he has the avians under control.
7. Business Updates:
    7.1 Beardy: Beardy stated that he was sorry to hear about the tax issues but would gladly step up to the mark. He also agrees that the perimeter area should not be closed. Monitored yes, but not closed. Surely we need some visitor types in the garden area, otherwise who's going to eat the worms and snails? Ada stated that she was partial to the odd snail but couldn't eat a whole garden's worth. Beardy also said that of course, would will look after Rosie.

7.2 Spencer: Spencer argued that the Chair is only delaying matters, and the closure of the perimeter area is inevitable. He also stated that he is more than capable of Chairing Tuesday's meeting. He also asked, is this the same Rosie who stayed with us before when times were less stressful? The Chair stated that it was the same Rosie. Spencer also asked was Rosie staying for the same reasons as the last time. The Chair stated that was also correct.

7.3 Horny Frank: Horny Frank stated that the last time Rosie was here if he remembered correctly, she wasn't completely satisfied with her visit! Although we can't blame Beardy entirely, as he lacked the necessary qualifications for such an operation, but hopes that valuable lessons were learnt and the same mistakes will not be repeated. The Chair agreed that the last visit was less than successful, but the same arrangements will apply this time. Beardy stated that the last time wasn't his fault; he was under a lot of pressure, especially with everybody watching, it was hard! Horny Frank argued yes, but it could've been harder for just a bit longer! Beardy argued that that was because when everybody wasn't watching, he got himself ever so excited! Horny Frank stated that apparently that can happen when you get ahead of yourself, that's why he thinks that he should look after Rosie this time, guaranteed happy ending, at the end, not before the beginning! The Chair thanked Horny Frank for volunteering his services but reiterated that it's non-negotiable, that's what the Stakeholder requested, Beardy has to look after Rosie, but hopefully with better outcomes this time. Horny Frank stated that he has been giving Beardy some *valuable lessons* in the art of looking after Rosie and will continue to do so.

7.4 Ada: Ada stated that she had conducted some black ops in the railway verge area. I've started mingling with the natives to try and collect some Intel. She said that she doesn't have much Intel at the moment but gets the feeling something big is going down. Beardy stated that he thinks the Big Foreign Bird's sudden appearance was a false flag event, plus, he added, there's that sudden 'time change' malarkey, strange times are afoot. Ada asked if Beardy thinks that the Big Foreign Bird was a crisis actor? She advised Beardy to stick with receiving valuable lessons from Horny Frank and should focus on his up and coming booty call.

7.5 Spud: Spud stated that he had nothing more to add.

8. Other business – None

10. THE INTERVIEW

10th Lockdown Board Meeting: Mon, 30th March 2020

In Attendance:

Me (Chair)

Spud II (Head of cat dept)

Spencer (Head of bigger dog dept)

Ada (Head of smaller dog dept)

Horny Frank (Head of horny rabbit dept)

Beardy (Head of not so horny rabbit dept)

Apologies - None

Call to order 06:00hrs

1. There were sufficient members for a quorum
2. Minutes of previous meeting approved
3. Business from last meeting: Rosie the white rabbit will arrive tomorrow and stay on Wednesday as well.

4. Statement from the Chair: Deputy CMO Dr Jenny stated that it could take six months to get back to normal, so that's not so good. Boris stated that 20,000 former NHS staff have returned to work, and 750,000 members of the public have volunteered to help out, so that's good.
5. Announcement from the Chair: He reiterated that there would be no business reporting today, as we have the members' statements for the Acting Chair position.
6. Members Statements:
   6.1 Spud: My name is Spud and currently Head of the cat department. I am a confident, reliable and enthusiastic cat. I enjoy informing our Stakeholders on a regular basis, and I am a face to face type of a cat. I strive to operate well under pressure and love to keep myself clean. I love hanging about watching things. I have currently taken on the role as Special Agent responsible for avian control of the garden area, which is completely under control. I would not change anything in any way as I believe we currently run a tight ship. Vote Spud and remember, patience is not the ability to wait. Thank you.
   6.2 Spencer: My name is Spencer and currently Head of the big dog department and joint Head of the Special Dog Branch. My primary duty is to keep the Board members safe at all costs, especially in the garden area. We currently live in perilous times, and I believe my constant surveillance work is fundamental. If I was Chair for a day, I would close the contentious perimeter area and relax the kitchen door policy with immediate effect. Vote Spencer who is keeping what's yours, yours. Thank You.
   6.3 Horny Frank: My name is Horny Frank, and I'm Head of the horny rabbit department. Horny by name, horny by nature as they say. I see myself as an educator and a great communicator? If I need to communicate stuff I can. I can talk the talk, and I am very talkative. I strive well under pressure and can contain myself for long periods of time, especially when required by the Stakeholders. I love to keep my workflow flowing, combined with true dedication, and I just wanna keep my customers satisfied. Vote Horny Frank, if you're too quick today, slow down tomorrow. Thank you.
   6.4 Ada: My name is Ada, and I'm Head of the small dog department and Head of Black Operations, unfortunately due to the official secrets act, I can't divulge any further information. I've been a member of the Board now for ten days and a member of the World for six months. This high

level of experience, along with my friendly and approachable persona, helps me support my fellow members, but don't be fooled because I will use my black ops skills, like jumping, and hole biting, when the need arises. I would close the perimeter area, but on top of that, claim a bit of the railway verge area and build a holding area where we can contain some visitor types, and there's no need for stakeholder updates on the holding area, as it's not technically in the garden area, so no *extra* reporting is needed if you get my drift? Vote Ada, where piece of mind is a matter of choice. Thank you.

    6.5 Beardy: My name is Beardy, and I'm Head of the not so horny rabbit department. I'm here to express my interest in the position of acting Chair. As a permanent Board member, I feel I would be a valuable asset to the Stakeholders. Not an asset like Ada, just the ordinary kind of asset. I have a wealth of experience in some areas and not so much in other areas, but I am bridging the gap with regular valuable lessons from Horny Frank. I'm very good with the Stakeholders and generally rise to the occasion- some of the time. If I was Chair for the day, I would organise a wee parade around the garden area, to show appreciation for the achievement of a reasonably respectful working environment. Vote Beardy because there's more to me than what you see. Thank you.

7. Other business – The Chair thanked the members for their statements and said that he would make his decision tonight and inform the members as soon as possible, so that the new acting Chair can prepare for tomorrow's business updates.

11. ROSIE PAYS A VISIT

11th Lockdown Board Meeting: Tues, 31st March 2020

In Attendance:

Spud II (Acting Chair and Head of cat dept)

Spencer (Head of bigger dog dept)

Ada (Head of smaller dog dept)

Horny Frank (Head of horny rabbit dept)

Beardy (Head of not so horny rabbit dept)

Apologies - Me (Chair)

Call to order 06:00hrs

1. There were sufficient members for a quorum
2. Minutes of previous meeting approved
3. Statement from Chair: The Government says - stay at home and save lives, except for Boris's best mate Dominic, so that's very interesting. University of Westminster's Dr Adele stated that washing your hands is important, so that's informative. Johnny

Vegas volunteers to deliver food in St Helens, so that's good. Russell Crowe thanks Johnny Vegas but warns the people of St Helens to count their biscuits, so that's informative.

4. Business from last meeting: Rosie the white rabbit will arrive today and stay on Wednesday as well.
5. Announcement from the Chair: Spud was the successful candidate, and he will Chair today's lockdown Board meeting, and further meetings should the need arise.
6. Business Updates:

    6.1 Spud (Acting Chair): The Acting Chair thanked everyone and stated that Rosie will be visiting us today and that we should be on our best behaviour, especially Beardy. The extra hutch has been set up now, and this will be Horny Frank's abode for the next couple of days. Rosie will share the main hutch with Beardy. Spud also stated that yesterday we received a communication from Boris in the form of a letter. In this letter, Boris said that he was still feeling a bit off, and that life in the country has changed dramatically, and action is absolutely necessary, because our wonderful NHS may not cope! But Boris has built a Dirty Place up Town for the sick humans to go to, but for some reason he's named it after an avian! Anyway said Spud, that's about it from Boris, apart from the usual, don't break the new rules, sorry you've no jobs, right measures right time, he's on the level, stay in and save lives, get out and save lives, we'll beat it together.

    6.2 Spencer: Spencer congratulated Spud on his appointment and appreciates the worsening times ahead. Maybe we should we send a representative to the Dirty Place up Town? The Acting Chair argued that that wasn't a good idea. It's dirty; it's in the name! He also stated that it would take him days of constant licking to get clean after such a visit. Spencer stated that we should do something for the sick humans, even Boris says, 'get out and help save lives,' let's face it without them we would never get cuddles nor walks again, and not to mention food! The Acting Chair stated that we will not be sending a representative to the Dirty Place up Town and said to Spencer that he needs to be a bit more self-sufficient and grow another pair.

    6.3 Horny Frank: Horny Frank argued that paying a visit to the Dirty Place up Town is actually a good idea. Humans who are poorly do like a bit of animal company; we soothe them apparently. In fact, rumour has it that we actually know when they're sick, so that has to be a good thing, the humans need us. Beardy agreed with Horny Frank, but was concerned about how they would even get there? Horny Frank suggested that they could follow the railway verge area towards up Town, and he's sure there'll be signs for the Dirty Place up Town the closer you get to up Town. Horny Frank also stated that he believes that he might be of better value if he cohabitated the main hutch with both Beardy and Rosie, so he could monitor the proceedings and advise accordingly, even jump in if required. Acting Chair stated that he had been given strict orders not to let Horny Frank get within smelling distance of Rosie. Horny Frank stated that he thought keeping a smelling distance was just a bit over the top, and not even logistically possible; he said that he can even smell her now and she isn't here yet! The Acting Chair stated that Horny Frank was to stay two meters from Rosie at all times and that it would help save Horny Frank's life.

6.4 Ada: Ada also congratulated Spud and stated that she always knew Boris was a bit off. However, she appreciates the letter and acknowledges the call for action. She said that she will increase black ops in the railway verge area and if a state of emergency is called, she will have no choice but to detain all visitor types that look a bit dodgy, like walking around for no reason. She also stated that a visit to the Dirty Place up Town is too dangerous at the moment, and even the railway verge area is becoming unsafe, there's far too many visitor types there now.

6.5 Beardy: Beardy stated that he welcomes the new arrangements and hopes that he won't let the side down with regards to Rosie's visit. He also stated that he volunteers to go to the Dirty Place up Town, after all, Boris says 'go out and help save lives.' Beardy also stated that he finds it strange that the Dirty Place up Town was named after an avian, it's obviously some sort of code from Boris. Ada stated that Beardy had enough on his plate over the next couple of days, plus Boris also said, 'stay in and save lives.' Spencer agreed with Ada and stated that Beardy would be stressed enough with all of us watching him carry out his duties with Rosie. The Acting Chair reiterated that there will be no visits to the Dirty Place up Town, and agreed that Beardy should use his time better and get a couple of valuable lessons in before Rosie gets here, and focus on trying to make lives.

7. Other business – None

12. BEARDY'S MISUNDERSTANDING

12th Lockdown Board Meeting: Wed, 1st April 2020

In Attendance:

Me (Chair)

Spud II (Head of cat dept)

Spencer (Head of bigger dog dept)

Ada (Head of smaller dog dept)

Horny Frank (Head of horny rabbit dept)

Beardy (Head of not so horny rabbit dept)

Apologies - None

Call to order 06:00hrs

1. There were sufficient members for a quorum
2. Minutes of previous meeting approved

3. Business from last meeting: None
4. Statement from the Chair: Mr T stated that there would be painful weeks ahead, so that's not good. Boris's mate Michael admitted that the country had to go further and faster to increase testing, so that's interesting. Boris's other mate Matt is urging hospitals to do much more, so that's interesting too.
5. Announcement from the Chair: The Chair thanked Spud for his help yesterday and said it was a job well done. The Chair was glad that he and the Stakeholders made the right choice.
6. Business Updates:
    6.1 Spud: Spud thanked the Chair for the opportunity and hoped he sorted the tax issue. The Chair stated he did sort the tax out, so that was good. Spud also said that during his watch, Rosie's visit was not quite sorted out yet, due to a few technical problems. Horny Frank stated that, in his defence, the 'valuable lessons' he gave to Beardy were technically correct and can't understand why Beardy couldn't carry those techniques forward and use them productively during Rosie's visit, even if a few minor adjustments were required. Beardy stated that he had done everything he was taught during the 'valuable lessons.' He also stated that any potential minor adjustments should've been made clear in advance of Rosie's visit.
    6.2 Ada: Ada argued that it's hard to train somebody who eats their own doo-doo. Horny Frank stated that there's no need to get personal; Beardy's eating habits have nothing to do with his lack of ability in sorting out Rosie's visit. Beardy thanked Horny Frank and stated that he has a dodgy belly and needs to eat things a couple of times over, sometimes even three times over. Ada argued that it's still weird and that she would rather starve than eat her own doo-doo!
    6.3 Horny Frank: Horny Frank stated that he probably needs to adjust the valuable lesson plan for the valuable lessons. Horny Frank added that Beardy just took his valuable lessons literally and suggested that Beardy might be on the Spectrum! Horny Frank reiterated that he said it before and he'll say again, he needs to be in there with Beardy to point out the pitfalls, show him the nooks and crannies in real-time. Look on the bright side, at least it wasn't a timing issue this time, replied Ada. Ada suggested that maybe during the valuable lessons they should reverse roles because that would be a valuable lesson worth watching. Horny Frank stated that he also has a kitchen door policy which will never be relaxed!

6.4 Spencer: Spencer suggested that maybe Horny Frank is right, and he should be allowed into the main hutch, purely on a consulting basis of course, with no crossing of swords, but only to point Beardy in the direction of the cranny. The Chair argued that it would be far too risky, the Stakeholder would be extremely unhappy with the type of result should it go wrong. Beardy just needs better valuable lessons which takes into consideration Beardy's special needs. Spencer stated that he had watched both the valuable lessons and the Rosie visit and Beardy was doing exactly the same thing both times. Ada suggested that maybe diagrams could prove useful, especially of the nooks and crannies.

6.5 Beardy: Beardy stated that he could assure everyone that his failure with Rosie's visit wasn't because he's on the Spectrum or because he eats his own doo-doo! He just ever so slightly misunderstood the context. He is now aware of the discrepancy, and does not need any more valuable lessons, ever again! Beardy added that he now has a good understanding of nooks and crannies and doesn't need diagrams either. Beardy also stated that although the Stakeholder wouldn't be happy with Rosie's visit at the moment, Rosie was in fact reasonably happy with the visit, from her point of view that is. That was of course, Beardy's point of view at the time, which was pretty much low-down chin on the ground and eyes forward. The Chair stated that the Stakeholder takes priority and as much as we have to appreciate Rosie's visit from Rosie's point of view, which should have been Beardy's point of view in the first place, we should continue with Rosie's visit and get it right this time.

7. Other business – None

13. BEARDY IS BANG ON

13th Lockdown Board Meeting: Thurs, 2nd April 2020

In Attendance:

Me (Chair)

Spud II (Head of cat dept)

Spencer (Head of bigger dog dept)

Ada (Head of smaller dog dept)

Horny Frank (Head of horny rabbit dept)

Beardy (Head of not so horny rabbit dept)

Apologies - None

Call to order 06:00hrs

1. There were sufficient members for a quorum
2. Minutes of previous meeting approved
3. Business from last meeting: None
4. Statement from the Chair: The NHS workers insist on getting tested, so that's reasonable. Boris stated that he's been saying for weeks and weeks, that testing is - how they will unlock the puzzle, so that's good. Dr Yvonne from PHE has stated that there is now the capacity for 3000 tests per day for NHS workers, and also said that her priority is to prioritise the priorities, so that's good too.
5. Announcement from the Chair: The Chair stated that spring finally arrived and so did Beardy. The Rosie visit was a success, and the Stakeholder was very happy, and he wanted to thank everyone involved, and that Rosie had now gone home.
6. Business Updates:
    6.1 Ada: Ada stated that she was glad that Rosie's visit was successful; she did look somewhat rather chipper when she left. Ada also said that she was concerned that some visitor types had entered the garden area via the decking area. She hasn't seen them yet but can smell them. It's obvious that there will be a battle underground soon, Ada added. Therefore, she might have to go under the decking area herself to investigate further and might need some assistance from the Chair. The Chair stated that he would not make an opening in the decking! If she wants in, she had to find her own way in.
    6.2 Spencer: Spencer stated that if there is visitor type activity under the decking area, then he agrees with Ada's underground investigation plan. He suggested that she might have to build a new containment facility under the decking area. Ada argued that the long tails would still be held officially within the garden area and we'd have to be nice to them and feed them etc. She suggested moving them straight to the railway verge area containment facility; that way we keep it off the books. Beardy asked, do you not feed the visitor types at the railway verge area containment facility? Ada stated that the visitors are fed, but it's only Subway leftovers chucked from the passing trains, not our Pets at Home gear, we just can't spare any during these stressful times, and now that the stressful times are getting worse over the next couple of weeks we can't be getting soft. Spencer asked if the Chair would he re-consider relaxing the kitchen

door policy now that the stressful times are getting worse. The Chair stated that even if Boris implements curfews and shuts down the networks before Easter, the kitchen door policy will not change.

6.3 Spud: Spud stated that he is sure the new visitor types are long tails, creepy little sneaky crawly type visitors. The Chair interrupted, he just remembered, could Spud please stop drinking from the bathroom toilet! It's not actually the drinking that's the problem; it's his hair, it's all over the place, even on the toothbrushes! It's bad enough with Her Indoors' hair all over the place, even on the toothbrushes! But ironically, Her Indoors is giving him grief over Spud's! Anyway, please stop, it'll make his life easier. Beardy stated that Spud had the cheek of making fun of him eating his own doo-doo and he's been drinking pee-pee all along. Spud argued that the water is fresh when he drinks it, and it's cleaner than the water from the communal drinking bowl, which is usually full of dog stuff! He stated that he used to have his own private ceramic automatic electric circulating water filtered fountain dish, then one day it was gone, then nothing, not a word, no explanation! The Chair stated that it stopped working, and now that we're in these stressful times Spud will have to make do. Spud argued that that's exactly what he was doing in the bathroom. The Chair stated that when these stressful times are over, we will invest in a new filtered fountain dish for the kitchen area.

6.4 Beardy: Beardy stated that he was pleased that the Rosie visit was successful, and now that he knows the right point of view, future visits should be less dramatic. He also added that he heard that the long tails just come in for a chat of an evening with the foxes. He stated that he hears the foxes chattering at night, they get their information from Karen, and a long tail called Ben. Spencer asked who Karen was? Beardy said he wasn't sure, but the foxes seem to think she's a sheep. Beardy asked the Chair, with regards to the very successful Rosie visit, was there a financial transaction of any kind? The Chair stated that remuneration was offered, however, he also said that he was offered first pick of the litter instead. Any money received will of course, go to our new Foundation, the Chair added. Horny Frank suggested that a permanent doe would be a wonderful addition. Beardy agreed that a permanent doe would be very advantageous long term, and he also stated that he hoped the new Foundation's accounts are visible and not subject to preferential rules on some island somewhere.

6.5 Horny Frank: Horny Frank stated that he was very sad Rosie had to go and hope she visits again soon, or even better, we get to enjoy the addition of a permanent doe. He also asked if there's a loss of networks, how will the Stakeholders receive our updates? The Chair stated that we'd cross that bridge if and when it comes.

7. Other business – None

14. BLOCKED KITCHEN DOOR

14th Lockdown Board Meeting: Fri, 3rd April 2020

In Attendance:

Me (Chair)

Spud II (Head of cat dept)

Spencer (Head of bigger dog dept)

Ada (Head of smaller dog dept)

Horny Frank (Head of horny rabbit dept)

Beardy (Head of not so horny rabbit dept)

Apologies - None

Call to order 06:00hrs

1. There were sufficient members for a quorum
2. Minutes of previous meeting approved
3. Business from last meeting: None

4. Statement from the Chair: Boris's mate Matt pledges to ensure that 100,000 people a day are tested by the end of the month, so that's very interesting. Boris's mate Matt also talked last night about green shoots, so that's odd. Boris is writing off £13.4b of NHS debt, so that's good.
5. Business Updates:
   5.1 Ada: Ada stated that she had no access to the garden area during the night because the cat flap was deliberately blocked with a mop bucket! The Chair stated that he could only apologise for this and the culprit was Her Indoors. Her Indoors said that Ada was making a hell of a racket last night, running in and out, barking all over the show. Apparently, it was very annoying, so when Ada came in, Her Indoors blocked the cat flap with the mop bucket. Ada argued that it is crucial that the cat flap is left open at night during these stressful times, which is the current policy, and the Chair will have to explain that to Her Indoors. The Chair asked is that why Ada left a little smelly parcel on the kitchen area floor last night? Ada stated that it was and that with every action there's always a smelly reaction. Ada stated that she would normally coil some rope when she goes on her last round, out by the perimeter area, but last night she couldn't because of the blocked cat flap and when you have to go, you have to go. Her Indoors didn't think about Ada having to go now did she, added Ada.
   5.2 Spud: Spud stated that he agreed, blocking the flap was definitely a boot in the hole offence, he couldn't get out last night either. In saying that, Spud added, he would not lay a cable on the kitchen floor area, that's just wrong. Ada argued that you have to stand your ground, sometimes a dirty protest is required. To be honest, Spud continued, he ended up sleeping with Her Indoors all night, lovely and cosy it was too, couldn't get out to hunt long tails, so did the next best thing, sleep. Her Indoors isn't that bad when she's sound asleep.
   5.3 Spencer: Spencer stated that it's getting ridiculous, how can we keep the visitor types out of the garden area at night when Her Indoors is taking it upon herself to close all access points without discussing it with the Board, we do have operating procedures in place! Her Indoors definitely requires a boot in the hole. The Chair stated that there's a boot in the hole policy between Her Indoors and the Chair which says - The Chair will not boot Her Indoors in the hole, and Her Indoors will not use a Black and Decker power tool on the Chair's kitchen

door while he's asleep. However, the Chair added, if Her Indoors blocks the cat flap at night again, and Ada pushes out another grumpy on the kitchen floor as a dirty protest, Her Indoors can clean it up, and Ada will definitely get a serious boot in the hole.

5.4 Horny Frank: Horny Frank stated that there was loads of activity in the garden area last night, the foxes were running amok. He stated that we need to clamp down heavily on all potential visitor types now, they're getting under the decking area, they're all over the railway verge area. Let's round a load up and give them what for. Beardy argued that maybe we should be more relaxed during these stressful times, maybe there's some good visitor types out there, not the foxes or the long tails of course, but surely a mole is ok for example? Ada reminded Beardy that this isn't Wind in the Willows, it's a War on Evil.

5.5 Beardy: Beardy stated that Ada should sign up to *victims.com*. Beardy added that maybe these stressful times are a way for us to understand how complacent we have all been? See how we miss all the simple things now? Possibly when these stressful times are over, we will all be happier and a lot friendlier toward visitor types. Save yourself first, Beardy insisted. If you're waiting for someone to save you, you're waiting for the snake. Look, said Ada, you can sit there in front of a mirror searching for yourself to save if you want, I'm going out to hunt me down some long tails and give them what for.

6. Other business – None

15. DR BEARDY'S NOO-NOO PROGNOSIS

15th Lockdown Board Meeting: Sat, 4th April 2020

In Attendance:

Me (Chair)

Spud II (Head of cat dept)

Spencer (Head of bigger dog dept)

Ada (Head of smaller dog dept)

Horny Frank (Head of horny rabbit dept)

Beardy (Head of not so horny rabbit dept)

Apologies - None

Call to order 06:00hrs

1. There were sufficient members for a quorum
2. Minutes of previous meeting approved

3. Business from last meeting: None
4. End of Week Statement from the Chair: We have been in lockdown now for two weeks. I'd want to thank all the departments for their cooperation during these stressful times. Our Stakeholders are still happy with our updates as they're probably all as crazy as we are, so we will continue until further notice. From what I gather, the situation with the human flu grows worse, and it's quite possible that further restrictions could be enforced.
5. Statement from the Chair: The BBC announced yesterday that a city in China have stopped eating cats, so that's gotta be good. The Guardian warns that Boris's mate Matt's pledge to test 100,000 people a day is - unravelling, so that's not so good. The NHS lab staff have stated that they don't have the chemicals and components they need to meet the testing target, so that's not good either.
6. Announcement from the Chair: We will conduct a feedback process starting today. All the Board members and the extras will be assessed by our Stakeholders and their furry friends via a poll on their performances over the last two weeks. Our Stakeholders will cast their vote our community page: https://www.facebook.com/groups/680667366014480/?ref=bookmarks. Please note that there will not be a postal vote.
The Chair and the Stakeholders believe that this will improve Board performance, as it will help evaluate different perspectives of their performances. This evaluation process will last for one week with the highest performer named on Sat, 11th April. The Chair will give a daily update on the current leaders.
7. Business Updates:
    7.1 Spud: Spud stated that he's shocked that humans eat cats, and asked, were cows and chickens not enough? Spencer stated it's not just the China humans that eat cats, and it's not only cats either, lots of human types eat long tails and the little green jumpers as well, apparently they're excellent cooked with a bit of garlic. Ada argued that long tails are very tasty, although she likes her meat raw as it's high in vitamin B. Spencer stated that he doesn't like cat meat himself but believes some human types see it as a good warm food during the winter months. Spencer stated that he's off fresh meat anyway, at the moment he prefers his meat highly processed with loads of sugar, no vitamins at all, especially Butchers lamb with rice and peas, it's like the McDonalds for dogs- Big Mac Butchers all the way.
    7.2 Beardy: Beardy stated that although he agrees with the concept of performance assessment, he's concerned that the

assessors may not be adequately trained to evaluate rabbits. Most Stakeholders tend to favour cats and dogs as their furry friends, while a mere 1% favour cute little bunnies, bunnies are right down there with indoor long tails and indoor avians, how can that be fair? The Chair stated that the Stakeholders will judge fairly and will not be biased and will only judge you on your performance during the Board meetings. That doesn't help, Beardy argued, dog lovers will vote dogs, cat lovers will vote cats etc., it's the nature of the beast.

7.3 Horny Frank: Horny Frank stated that 'performance' was his second name. Stakeholders are only interested in the delivery of outcomes; they don't care if you're an indoor avian or an indoor long tail, you produce the goods the right way, at the right time, you're getting the points. It doesn't even have to be the right way either, so bring it on. Horny Frank also stated that he was pleased that the rabbit departments received a special gift yesterday, a carrot-topped cottage to gnaw on, obviously, Pets at Home are getting back to normal. The Chair stated that Her Indoors was doing the monthly visit to Pets at Home and got a few extra bits. Spencer stated that Her Indoors was probably feeling guilty about the cat flap incident as the big dog department received a new bed too. The Chair stated that Her indoors never feels guilty about anything ever and that Spencer needed a new bed as Ada had a habit of leaking on it. Ada stated that she only leaks a little when she gets excited or stressed and that that type of leak isn't a boot in the hole offence. The Chair agreed that Ada's little leaks couldn't be helped. Beardy suggested that Ada needs a noo-noo sling.

7.4 Ada: Ada thanked Dr Beardy for his noo-noo prognosis and stated that instead of worrying about her neck of bladder, he should be more concerned about his neck of head. She also reminded Beardy that raw rabbit meat is a good source of vitamin B too.

7.5 Spencer: Spencer stated that he plans on doing a leaflet drop further up the railway verge area; offering a reward for handing over suspicious visitor types. Ada agreed with Spencer and stated that this was an excellent idea. Spencer stated that we might need to build an extension to our containment facility; buy loads of cigarettes. Beardy stated that he didn't know Spencer smoked. Spencer said he doesn't and what a bizarre thing to think.

8. Other business – None

16. CRISPY DRY TIME IS A THING

16th Lockdown Board Meeting: Sun, 5th April 2020

In Attendance:

Me (Chair)

Spud II (Head of cat dept)

Spencer (Head of bigger dog dept)

Ada (Head of smaller dog dept)

Horny Frank (Head of horny rabbit dept)

Beardy (Head of not so horny rabbit dept)

Apologies - None

Call to order 06:00hrs

1. There were sufficient members for a quorum
2. Minutes of previous meeting approved
3. Business from last meeting: None

4. Statement from the Chair: The new Nightingale hospital has been officially opened by Charlie boy and it's going to hold up to 4000 patients, so that's good. Boris's mate Matt stated that this invisible killer is stalking the whole world, so that's not so good. The Queen will make an announcement tonight and thank the NHS staff and key workers, so that's nice.
5. Best performer: Currently, Ada leads the performance pack.
6. Business Updates:
    6.1 Spud: Spud stated that he is going to have a very chilled weekend. It's a lovely weekend, the sun's out, what could be better than to sit and watch others work or isolate themselves in a park. Ada reminded Spud about the War on Evil, and we shouldn't let our guard down, where's the Big Foreign Bird for example, what's she up to? Ada stated that she thinks the Big Foreign Bird is a spook, wandering about spooking things up like spooks do. Beardy asked do Spooks call themselves Spooks and do Spooks work for the invisible killer? The Chair stated probably not on both accounts but who knows these days.
    6.2 Beardy: Beardy asked wasn't Charlie boy sick? The Chair stated very much so, but Charlie boy wasn't there in person, he was in Scotland, he opened the Dirty Place up Town from a TV. That's great, said Beardy, science is a wonderful thing. How many sick humans are currently at the Dirty Place up Town? continued Beardy. The Chair stated that there were none at the moment, but hopefully, they will have six by the end of the next week, which was good. Beardy asked would the doctors and nurses be doing a wee dance for TikTok? Most probably, replied the Chair.
    6.3 Horny Frank: Horny Frank asked what his current position in the ratings was. The Chair stated that Horny Frank was currently in 5th place. Early days yet, Horny Frank replied. Horny Frank noticed that during these stressful times, and especially when the sun is out, the Chair seems to be drinking more and more wine. He also lights that stupid wood burner thing, which stinks, and the smoke is all over the place, and it follows you around, you can't escape it! The Chair stated that when he's done his work for the day, he likes to relax with a glass of wine with the lovely smell of burning peat in the air, listening to a bit of music, it's the best way to spend an afternoon. Ada argued that the Chair is usually sound asleep by the afternoon. The Chair explained that his afternoons start early and finish early. Spencer added that if anything happens

to the Chair, then the Board would be left to Her Indoors to manage and that can't be good. Beardy argued that that wouldn't be the worst thing in the world, she does like to shop a lot, and she does get us goodies, the Chair never thinks about getting us goodies. Anyway, the Chair added, a few drops of wine a day didn't hurt anybody. You tell them Georgie boy, replied Ada.

6.4 Ada: Ada stated, anyway enough of the 12 steps stuff, these avians are back, tweeting their little tweets off. Tweeting should be banned from the air. As soon as they wake up in the morning, they start tweeting, then another starts tweeting back. Then thousands of tweets, all making the same stupid useless sound. Now Spud decides to go on a go-slow weekend, Ada continued, laying there under his favourite bush with his wee sun-kissed cat face, we need action, and we need it now. Beardy suggested that Ada was getting a bit ratty, no offence to the long tails, but was this really a good time for a call to action when she's in a wee ratty mood. Horny Frank interrupted and stated that that reminds him, how come the Chair doesn't drink red wine? The Chair said that he relaxes with a dry white, it suits the afternoons better, crispy and dry.

6.5 Spencer: Spencer stated that to be honest, this lockdown has taken its toll. Especially with the Chair's crispy dry afternoons becoming a thing. He's starting to miss our feeding times, and we can't rely on Her Indoors, so he needs to get his act together. A suggestion would be to do the food run early in the afternoon, say 10:00hrs and fill the bowls with a full day's worth. The Chair stated that the feeding times would remain the same, approximately. Spencer also noted that Ada went missing for a while, and nobody seemed to be bothered! The Chair asked Ada to explain. Ada stated that she was in deep black ops in the railway verge area when she spotted what looked like Ben the Long Tail. She wasn't sure it was Ben the Long Tail as they all look alike, but definitely a long tail. She followed him into an alien garden area where she was immediately met by hostiles. Nasty looking human types ready to dish out some serious what for. The Chair asked if she recognised them? Ada stated that they were all wearing masks and armed with brooms. Spencer asked if they tortured her? Well, there was no chance of a cuddle from any of them, that's for sure, Ada replied. She waggled her tail like she never waggled it before with no effect, completely heartless, never felt so much hurt with abandonment before. Even when Her

Indoors yells at her for licking her face after she's cleaned Spencer's danger noodle, that was nothing compared to this.
7. Other business – None

17. KAREN THE SHEEP SHOWS UP

17th Lockdown Board Meeting: Mon, 6th April 2020

In Attendance:

Me (Chair)

Spud II (Head of cat dept)

Spencer (Head of bigger dog dept)

Ada (Head of smaller dog dept)

Horny Frank (Head of horny rabbit dept)

Beardy (Head of not so horny rabbit dept)

Apologies - None

Call to order 06:00hrs

1. There were sufficient members for a quorum
2. Minutes of previous meeting approved
3. Business from last meeting: None

4. Statement from the Chair: The Queen made her public announcement last night, she understands our financial difficulties during these stressful times, so that's good. The Scottish CMO Dr Calderwood, is completely immune to all rules, so that's handy. Boris's mate Matt is getting angry about people breaking the rules who aren't immune to the rules, like Dr Calderwood is, so that's interesting. Boris is in hospital, so that's not good.
5. Best performer: Currently, Ada leads the performance pack
6. Business Updates:
    6.1 Spud: Spud stated that it was another crispy dry afternoon yesterday. Sun was out, fires were lit, food-run missed, again! Spencer asked the Chair again to re-think the food-run time protocol. Spencer stated that it would be much better for all concerned to start the food-run before the afternoon's crispy dry time. It's very noticeable that the afternoon's crispy dry time starts spot on 10:30hrs, yet food-run times vary day by day, sometimes it doesn't even happen until night-time when Her Indoors gets home. The Chair stated that he can only apologise for his recent complacency during the crispy dry afternoons and will adjust the food-run time to 10:00hrs.
    6.2 Beardy: Beardy stated, on top of that, now that the dog walkies in the park have taken a back seat as well during these stressful times, there is an accumulation of dog doo-doo all over the garden area. Ada argued that all of the rabbit's hutch area is covered in rabbit doo-doo and that he had the cheek to talk. Beardy argued that that was his point exactly, nothing is getting done anymore. These may be stressful times, but no chores are taking place! The Chair is enjoying his crispy dry afternoon times in the morning, while the rest of us are wallowing in our own doo-doo. The Chair apologised once again and stated that he would endeavour to do a doo-doo-run just before the food-run in order to free up some garden area for that afternoon's doo-doo doings. The Chair stated that he would make it up to everybody by preparing some great food dishes for today. Nice one Gino, replied Ada.
    6.3 Spencer: Spencer stated that Karen the Sheep came close to the perimeter area yesterday afternoon, and it must be said that Karen the Sheep is one ugly sheep. Ada stated that she had to agree with Spencer, Karen the Sheep was wearing earrings that did nothing for her complexion. Beardy said that Karen the Sheep looked like a bloke sheep. What did Karen the Sheep want? Beardy continued. Spencer stated that she was just standing there chewing the cud, eyeing up our green

grass. Well she can go flock herself if she thinks she's eating our green grass stated Horny Frank. Spencer stated that Karen the Sheep didn't have a horn, which was good, nothing worse than an ugly sheep with a horn.

6.4 Ada: Ada stated that she recently noticed the lack of toys around the garden area, and she only has an old glove to play with. She added that she enjoys the old glove, but during these stressful times, she would like more of a variety. The Chair stated that he would pass that on to Her Indoors as she manages that type of stuff. The Chair also stated that he noticed that Ada was starting to roll around in dog doo-doo and ask could she could refrain from this practice. Ada stated that it's her camouflage, she said that she usually smells far too nice and the long tails know her smell. So, she started to mask her lovely smell with a bit of doo-doo. Surely that's not a boot in the hole offence Ada asked. The Chair stated that it might not be a boot in the hole offence, but night-time cuddles in front of the TV are off the menu for sure. Plus, you'll be hosed down before being allowed back in the kitchen area.

6.5 Horny Frank: Horny Frank asked what his current position in the ratings was. The Chair stated that Horny Frank was still currently in 5th place. Still early days replied Horny Frank. Horny Frank stated that during yesterday's crispy dry event, the Chair was playing Shakin Stevens songs. It's incredibly irritating having to listen to just one Shakin Stevens song but having an album on repeat was far too much. The Chair stated that he had dosed off for bit while he was sunbathing. Ada stated that the Chair had dosed off for three albums worth! The Chair stated that his face was sunburnt all over, except for a wee dog's face type shape on his right cheek! Ada stated that she's sorry, it was her, while the Chair was having his wee crispy dry sleep she snuggled into his cheek and kept it cool with a bit of serious licking. The Chair stated that he was having a lovely wee dream about a BBC Breakfast News presenter.

7. Other business – None

18. KAREN THE SHEEP IS IN HIDING

18th Lockdown Board Meeting: Tues, 7th April 2020

In Attendance:

Me (Chair)

Spud II (Head of cat dept)

Spencer (Head of bigger dog dept)

Ada (Head of smaller dog dept)

Horny Frank (Head of horny rabbit dept)

Beardy (Head of not so horny rabbit dept)

Apologies - None

Call to order 06:00hrs

1. There were sufficient members for a quorum
2. Minutes of previous meeting approved
3. Business from last meeting: None

4. Statement from the Chair: Boris is getting sicker, he's in ITU at St Thomas' now, so that's not good. Boris's mate Raab is in charge, so that's good. Nadia, the big cat, has the virus, so that's not good.
5. Best performer: Currently, Ada leads the performance pack
6. Business Updates:
   6.1 Ada: Ada stated that she has been keeping a close eye on Karen the Sheep. She's still hanging around the railway verge area, by the old outhouse. She's in hiding, apparently from the rest of the sheep types. Ada added that the foxy fox was right; she is quite chatty. She was telling her that the globe is flat. Really, how can a globe be flat? asked Spencer. No idea, said Ada, but she's so convinced. She also stated that the human flu was a human flu copy, made in China, a cheaper human flu knock-off if you like. Definitely a good source of information, keep her close stated Spencer.
   6.2 Spud: Spud stated that that's all he needs, a new cat flu, and all the justification for measures that could come with it! The Chair stated that Nadia was in fact a tiger in New York, so that's good. Still, Spud argued, if it can happen there, it can happen anywhere. Horny Frank stated that Spud is having delusions of grandeur. You're missing the point, argued Horny Frank, Nadia is a tiger, not a house cat! Still, it's the same thing, argued Spud; we have the same number of teeth, we hunt the same, although the size of our dinners might be slightly different. Tigers can swim, and they have round pupils, added Horny Frank, so you're not quite the same.
   6.3 Spencer: Spencer stated that on the subject of Karen the Sheep, ugly as she is, she did have an excellent haircut. So, he was thinking; his hair was getting a tad long, and wondered when the next Penny visit was due? The Chair stated that because of the stressful times, he's not sure if Penny is currently cutting hairs. Spencer asked wasn't Penny, a key worker. The Chair stated that he doesn't think so, only doctors, nurses and apparently news reporters are key workers. Therefore, the Chair might have to cut Spencer's hair himself. Spencer asked if that was a wise move. The Chair stated that he'd watch a YouTube video, how hard can it be? Spencer asked, then could it be done in the morning time, as there's more of a chance that both the Chair's eyes will be working and communicating with each other.
   6.4 Beardy: Beardy stated that he was very impressed that the Chair produced some delightful snacks during the morning time. He appreciated that it was raining outside, and the crispy

dry thing was on hold, but a nice touch nonetheless. The Chair stated that there was a bit of Stakeholder pressure to be honest, they don't like starved animals apparently, so he was sorry about that. Ada stated that the long sausage-like things were delicious, what were they called? Spencer replied that they were called sausages. She couldn't believe it; she was lying there in the kitchen area minding her own, when the Chair came in, cooked a couple of those sausage things, and give her one! Plus, Ada added, the Chair walked past her another time, and just picked her up, and just cuddled her for no good reason at all, she couldn't contain herself, well actually she did contain herself, that would've been a very different ending had she not contained herself.

   6.5 Horny Frank: Horny Frank asked what his current position in the ratings was. The Chair stated that Horny Frank was now currently in 4th place. Now that's what he's talking about, added Horny Frank, he's on the move upwards. You won't get higher than that stated Spud. Horny Frank argued that Spud was just getting catty because he's not a sick tiger from New York. At least he wasn't a drunken afterthought like Horny Frank, stated Spud. Horny Frank was an afterthought? asked Ada. Yes, he sure was, both he and Beardy were, replied Spud. Do tell, insisted Ada. Well, continued Spud, you know Her Indoors likes to head out to the shops on a Saturday afternoon to do what she does best. Well, the Chair goes out with her but goes to the pub to do what he does best too. Well one particular sunny Saturday afternoon, Her Indoors got carried away and took a bit longer than usual doing what she does best. Therefore, the Chair was doing what he does best for a bit longer too. To cut a long story short, the Chair ended up pished. Anyway, Spud continued, Her Indoors had one more thing to do before going home, and that was to get Spud's program oral suspension from 'Pets at Home'. Well didn't the Chair go into the store as well, and the first thing he nearly saw was Beardy and Horny Frank and insisted on having them. Her Indoors just went along with it just for the craic, happy with just anticipating the look on the Chair's face the next morning when he wakes up. So Ada stated, if it wasn't for Spud's fleas, Beardy and Horny Frank would still be in a shop window. Exactly, said Spud, they're nothing but a pished afterthought!

7.   Other business – None

19. THEIR LITTLE HEARTS ARE BURSTING

19th Lockdown Board Meeting: Wed, 8th April 2020

In Attendance:

Me (Chair)

Spud II (Head of cat dept)

Spencer (Head of bigger dog dept)

Ada (Head of smaller dog dept)

Horny Frank (Head of horny rabbit dept)

Beardy (Head of not so horny rabbit dept)

Apologies - None

Call to order 06:00hrs

1. There were sufficient members for a quorum
2. Minutes of previous meeting approved
3. Business from last meeting: None

4. Statement from the Chair: Boris is stable and in good spirits, so that's good. The first patient has been admitted to the new Nightingale hospital, so that's good too. NHS spokesperson stressed that London hospitals have still not reached capacity yet, so that's interesting.
5. Best performer: Currently, Ada leads the performance pack
6. Business Updates:
    6.1 Ada: Ada stated that would it be possible for the Chair not to get them too excited when Her Indoors gets home from work in the evenings? Ada stated that the Chair does the same thing every night, we hear the car coming into the driveway, so it's exciting. But then the Chair keeps her and Spencer in the kitchen area with the door closed and starts saying things like, 'is that your mommy home,' 'is that your mommy home,' over and over again. It like drives us mad; we are beside ourselves with excitement, the Chair must see that our wee hearts are bursting. Spencer stated that it was very true, it's pandemonium, Ada is showing off her jumping skills and biting skills, she bites his legs when she gets over-excited. It's the same when it's time for a walk. The Chair says, 'who wants to go walkies,' over and over again, 'who wants to go walkies,' who wants to go walkies,' and to be fair, just saying 'walkies' once would suffice. But no, the Chair goes on and on, and then for a change he goes, 'where are we going,' 'where are we going.' Like why? The happiness is insane to start with, we know we're going out for walkies before you even utter the word, we smell it, so we have to question your intent! Are you manipulating our pure emotion for your own amusement?
    6.2 Spud: Spud stated that he doesn't see the fuss. Sometimes he can go days with not even knowing that Her Indoors had come home. Spencer stated, you say that, but when the Chair says 'who wants din-dins,' you start making that stupid cat sound and that pathetic thing you do with your eyes, it's the same thing. Spud stated that he begged to differ; he was just showing some appreciation for what he was about to receive. Even if they didn't feed you and Ada for a month, you'd still be overwhelmed with joy to see them; you'd empty your tanks, it's hardly the same. To be fair, Spencer stated, his sphincters are working perfectly, only Ada empties her tank involuntarily.
    6.3 Beardy: Beardy stated, to be honest, both rabbit departments only get a Royal visit once a month, usually with a goodie though, and although pleasant as it is, he doesn't get over-

excited, no tanks are emptied by mistake there. Can't even recall her face half the time. We see the Chair every day at these lockdown board meetings and hear him singing along to Shakin Stevens when the sun's out and the fire's lit, so we know him.

6.4 Horny Frank: Horny Frank asked what his current position in the ratings was. The Chair stated that Horny Frank was now currently in 3rd place, he just hopped ahead of Beardy. 'Up yours Spud!' said Horny Frank. Spud argued that he so didn't care. Horny Frank agreed that he'd be hard pushed to remember what Her Indoors looks like on a daily basis, definitely know when the Chair pays a visit to the hutch, he's the ham wallet with the camera.

6.5 Spencer: Spencer stated that Spud thinks he's a big tiger, out catching deer for dinner every day with his same amount of teeth, when in fact he actually prefers food dry from a packet and served up in his wee bowl, with a picture of a cat on it, so we all know it's 'his bowl', when in fact we don't know it's 'his bowl' at all, it's just another stupid bowl. Anyway, the Chair interrupted, you all know the routine, When Her Indoors gets home she doesn't want to see you lot right away because you'll only click her tights, and you end up with some serious boots in the hole. So, she gets her bath first, gets changed and then receives you for cuddles, then settles down to catch up with her soaps. The Chair can then sneak off to his man cave where he can catch up with re-runs of BBC Breakfast News, and maybe a drop of aqua vita to mark another happy ending.

7. Other business – None

20. ADA'S IN TROUBLE AGAIN

20th Lockdown Board Meeting: Thurs, 9th April 2020

In Attendance:

Me (Chair)

Spud II (Head of cat dept)

Spencer (Head of bigger dog dept)

Ada (Head of smaller dog dept)

Horny Frank (Head of horny rabbit dept)

Beardy (Head of not so horny rabbit dept)

Apologies - None

Call to order 06:00hrs

1. There were sufficient members for a quorum
2. Minutes of previous meeting approved
3. Business from last meeting: None

4. Statement from the Chair: Boris's mate Rishi stated that there's no end in sight, so that's not good. Boris's mate Rishi also stated that Boris is still in ITU, in an ITU bed, but he's sitting up talking, so that's good. Boris's cat Larry is fine too, so that's good too.
5. Best performer: Currently, Ada still leads the performance pack (Horny Frank is 3rd)
6. Business Updates:

    6.1 Beardy: Beardy stated that he was very disappointed with Ada yesterday. Her Indoors had a day off yesterday and decided to do a monthly on the hutch. This is usually a good thing, as they tend to get nice new wood shavings, the hutch is moved to a new grass area in the garden area, and they usually they some goodie stuff too. Yesterday was no exception; as a treat, they got their favourite carrot-cottage. Everything went swimmily well until Her Indoors had finished and left the garden area. She forgot to place the carrot-cottage in the hutch run! Her Indoors left it outside! Ada got it! Beardy and Horny Frank had to sit there and watch Ada destroy it! Beardy stated that they could make a carrot-cottage last 3-4 days, Ada had it wrecked within minutes. The Chair stated that Her Indoors was very sorry with regards to her role in the carrot-cottage incident and vowed to replace it whenever she gets a chance. Her Indoors also stated that she was very disappointed in Ada, but more disappointed in the Chair, as he very obviously watched it all unfold and did nothing. Ada stated that she thought it was her new toy that she had been promised for ages, and also said that anything in the garden area is fair game, even game. Spud stated that it's the same with his scratchy stretcher, Ada has it completely ruined too.

    6.2 Ada: Ada Stated that she had another meet up with Karen the Sheep. Karen the Sheep was hiding from the human flu. She watches lots of cat types wondering about not even keeping their distance and cats can now get the human flu and spread it. Ada stated that from the Intel she received from Karen the Sheep, she thinks all cats should be detained immediately, starting with Spud. Ada also indicated that she has cleared out the containment facility of all the long tails, as she couldn't feed them anymore, because the trains stopped going past and the scraps dried up and long tails were looking a bit on the thin side, so she released them. So, we have plenty of room to detain and isolate Spud, if required.

6.3 Spud: Spud stated that this was fake news and Ada shouldn't listen to misinformation from nut cases. The Chair said that only those who have the human flu with symptoms are self-isolating and should keep their cats indoors. Spud stated that it's all scaremongering and he bets that Boris's cat Larry isn't locked up. Ada stated that there was no harm in being careful, and insisted that while Spud was in detention, Ada would personally make sure that Spud gets food. Spud stated once again that this is scaremongering and there is no real evidence of cats spreading the human flu. Spud argued that Karen the Sheep is a railway verge area troll and is trying to sow discord within the garden area.

6.4 Horny Frank: Horny Frank stated last night that he heard foxy the fox talking about a conversation he had with Ben the Long Tail. Apparently, Ben the Long Tail heard from one of his other long tail types, that they were chatting to the Big Foreign Bird who just came back from visiting other places, where it was common knowledge that Spud gets food from human types from another garden area. Spud argued that this is a slur on his good name for political gain, and it's quite apparent now that Horny Frank is up to no good because Spud is above Horny Frank in the performance leader board, and Horny Frank wants to alienate Spud from the Stakeholders. Well, Spud continued, it won't work because at the end of the day, Spud's a cat and Horny Frank isn't. Spud added that at his very best Horny Frank will only ever achieve 3rd place at anything he ever does here because he's only a rabbit. Horny Frank stated that this was discriminatory language, almost hate talk, and suggests a social investigation is required.

6.5 Spencer: Spencer stated that the Chair's music was a bit better yesterday during his crispy dry time, he especially liked the wagon wheel song and the one about all those red balloons. However, Spencer also stated that it was another sunny day yesterday and noticed that the extra sausage treats were no longer available. He appreciated that the food-run was nearly on time yesterday but couldn't help but wonder, were the extra treats the other day just a PR stunt for the Stakeholders as they don't like animals being starved, and that the Chair was under pressure with the sudden outcry. The Chair stated that it was not a PR stunt and that the sausage man was furloughed.

7. Other business – None

21. ADA GET'S LOCKED UP

21st Lockdown Board Meeting: Fri, 10th April 2020

In Attendance:

Me (Chair)

Spud II (Head of cat dept)

Spencer (Head of bigger dog dept)

Ada (Head of smaller dog dept)

Horny Frank (Head of horny rabbit dept)

Beardy (Head of not so horny rabbit dept)

Apologies - None

Call to order 06:00hrs

1. There were sufficient members for a quorum
2. Minutes of previous meeting approved
3. Business from last meeting: None
4. Statement from the Chair: Good morning, it's Good Friday, so that's a good start. Boris is feeling better, so that's good too. Boris's dad Stanley is relieved that his son is in recovery and stated that - it

got the whole country to believe that this event is serious, so that's great.
5. Announcement from the Chair: Due to feedback from our Stakeholders, it was decided that Ada was to be punished for the destruction of the Carrot-Cottage. Therefore, when Beardy and Horny Frank were indoors spending some quality time yesterday, Ada was locked up in the rabbit hutch.
6. Best performer: Currently, Ada still leads the performance pack (Horny Frank is 3rd)
7. Business Updates:
    7.1 Ada: Ada stated that she was very unhappy with her incarceration yesterday and has made the following announcement: 'I was arrested late yesterday afternoon. I was locked up and now I've done my porridge. During my incarceration, I had no access to a victim liaison officer, so I've had to deal with this alone. I want to state for the record that the crime did not affect me at the time, nor does it affect me now. I would like to thank the support I received from the 'free the carrot-cottage one' pressure group, God bless you.'
    7.2 Beardy: Beardy asked that we should have a special celebration for rabbits over the coming festive weekend. Ada asked was Beardy going to hand out eggs on Sunday, and will they be proper chocolate eggs or just painted chicken type eggs? Beardy stated that he thought that maybe the Chair could give us Easter treats like wee Easter veggie sticks. Ada asked what Easter veggie sticks were. Beardy stated that they're veggie sticks you get at Easter. Ada asked were they made of chocolate or maybe do they smell like roast lamb? Beardy said no, just smell like veggies and probably made of plastic. Ada stated that she and Spencer get a Hatchwell's special, which at least resembles a chocolate Easter egg.
    7.3 Spud: Spud stated that it was mentioned during yesterday's Board meeting that cat owners who had the human flu with symptoms should keep their cats indoors. Spud asked that who actually owned him? Well, officially Spud is owned by Her Indoors, replied the Chair. Beardy asked if he and Horny Frank were owned by the Chair as he got them when he was pished or was he too much under the influence to be a responsible purchaser at the time, and therefore legally, are the responsibility of Her Indoors. The Chair stated that they were definitely his responsibility, even though he had no recollection of the purchase, he only remembers thinking that it would be great fun to have a rampant rabbit.

7.4 Horny Frank: Horny Frank stated that he didn't realise an Easter bunny was a rabbit thingy at Easter, he thought it was a sex position. Horny Frank added that we definitely should celebrate this rabbit festival and highlight the importance of rabbits. Rabbits have been in the shadows for far too long. Horny Frank stated that he hadn't been aware that rabbits were even celebrated, so he's seen the Light. Our Stakeholders very typically own cats and dogs, and that's obvious by all the cute little photographs they show, continued Horny Frank. Where are all the photographs of the Thumpers and Snowballs, it's time we bucked up. Horny Frank also stated that being a rabbit is like being left-handed, some have a rabbit, most don't, and nobody really knows why it's just the way it is. No one should be afraid to walk up the street holding a rabbit.

7.5 Spencer: Spencer asked who owned him. The Chair stated that he owned Spencer. Spencer asked was the Chair pished at the time he bought him. The Chair said no definitely not, but to be fair, he couldn't really remember. Ada asked who had bought her. The Chair stated that he had bought Ada, but as a Christmas present for Her Indoors, so officially Ada belongs to Her Indoors. So, asked Ada, was she a Christmas present then? Was she all wrapped up in a cute wee box with ribbons? Was she opened up first or was she left to the end as the main special pressie? Anyway, Spencer continued, in respect to some of our Stakeholders, maybe we should not eat meat today. Why on earth would you do that asked Spud. Well replied Spencer, to some human types, it's a Fast day. They're not wrong there, said Spud, it's 7 o'clock already!

8. Other business – Stakeholders are concerned about Spud II being called just Spud. The Chair asked for it to be on the agenda for the next meeting.

22. HER INDOORS FAVOURS HORNY FRANK

22nd Lockdown Board Meeting: Sat, 11th April 2020

In Attendance:

Me (Chair)

Spud II (Head of cat dept)

Spencer (Head of bigger dog dept)

Ada (Head of smaller dog dept)

Horny Frank (Head of horny rabbit dept)

Beardy (Head of not so horny rabbit dept)

Apologies - None

Call to order 06:00hrs

1. There were sufficient members for a quorum
2. Minutes of previous meeting approved

3. Business from last meeting: Some of our Stakeholders mentioned the fact that Spud is listed in the attendance section as Spud II, yet during the business updates section he is listed as Spud. The discrepancy seems to create two issues with our Stakeholders. 1 - Inconsistency, which shouts out complacency on the part of the scribe, and messes with our Stakeholders OCD. 2 - Re-use of the name Spud. Was there a Spud 1? Instead of coming up with a new name, the old name was suffice. The Chair met up with Spud/Spud II off-line and discussed this issue in detail. As a result, Spud/Spud II, has made the following announcement: 'I had no say in the choosing of my name whatsoever. I don't care what I'm called, call me Cat if you like, I really don't care. However, just to clear this issue up and deliver a resolution, I will keep my original full title as Spud II. This is purely for the sake of the vets, insurance documents and minute attendance records. However, I will identify myself as Spud at any other time. I hope our Stakeholders will understand and embrace my universal right to be both Spud II and Spud simultaneously, and not have any issues with inclusion and diversity. I don't know what OCD is, but it sounds nasty.'
4. End of the Week Statement from the Chair: We have been in lockdown now for three weeks. Reuters stated that infections and hospital admissions are starting to plateau, so that's very good. I want to thank all departments for their cooperation during these stressful times. Our mad but lovable Stakeholders are still happy with our updates, so we will continue.
5. Statement from the Chair: Boris's mate Matt stated that he is making a herculean effort to protect our NHS, so that's good. Boris's mate Priti stated that we are - taking the right steps at the right moment in time, so that's good too. Boris's mate Priti also stated that they are working day and night to get the resources needed, so that's great.
6. Best performer: The performance poll has ended for this week and Ada is Best Performer, and the Chair has given her a special toy. She had a few dodgy moments during the week, but our very wise Stakeholders pick her as the best.
7. Business Updates:
    7.1 Ada: Ada stated that she was thrilled that she's the Best, and also delighted with her new toy. Spencer said well done and asked her what the toy was. Ada stated that it was a wee black plastic thing the Chair bought her. What did it do? asked Spencer. It didn't do anything, replied Ada, the Chair just throws it, she chases after it and chews it. It's just fantastic. Ada also stated that she's been back out on black ops in the

railway verge area and had a brush-pass with Karen the Sheep, our agent-in-place. Karen the Sheep stated that there is a new pole in the railway verge area that wasn't there before, for the sole purpose in controlling us. Spencer asked Ada what the Pole was doing there, was he working? Ada stated the pole wasn't a he; it was a thing, a big long thing stuck in the ground. So it's a big long thing stuck in the ground to control sheep? asked Spencer. Apparently so replied Ada.

7.2 Beardy: Beardy stated that yesterday was a bit odd. Her Indoors was off work again and hanging around the hutch, making a racket cutting the grass and stuff. She was drinking all that fizzy stuff, and was to all tense and purposes, pished. Then when it was his and Horny Frank's time for quality time indoors, Her Indoors just took Horny Frank and left Beardy all on his own. What was that all about? Beardy asked, on our special Rabbit Festival weekend too. Horny Frank said that he was surprised also, and he didn't go indoors anyway, he was outdoors with Her Indoors at the Chair's crispy dry table. The Chair wasn't there, just Her Indoors, she said that Horny Frank was her favourite, and the cutest, and that he was the only one that understood her. The cuddles he got was unreal. And to be honest, said Horny Frank, he understood diddly squat. The Chair stated that Her Indoors has been very busy during these stressful times, and when she gets some time off, she likes to play with her favourite rabbit. Beardy asked if the Chair had a favourite rabbit. Don't be ridiculous, replied the Chair.

7.3 Spud: Spud stated that he was feeling poorly this morning. He has a high temperature, and he feels hot to touch on his chest and back. He has a new continuous cough and had several episodes of coughing over a 24hr period; ever since that big pole thing was stuck in the railway verge area. Oh dear God, really! cried Beardy. No, added Spud. he was just yanking their chains. The looks on their faces, priceless, laughed Spud.

7.4 Horny Frank: Horny Frank stated that he is delighted with the way the Rabbit Festival weekend was going, building up to Rabbit Day on Sunday. He noticed that the Stakeholders were showing photographs of their special rabbits. He'd like to give a special shout out to Bigwig, Alfie Babbit and Bondara for their contribution, very much appreciated. Horny Frank stated that he could tell there is a lot of bunny love out there at the moment.

7.5 Spencer: Spencer stated that Ada should be careful with regards to Karen the Sheep. Ada stated that she had the situation well under control. She thinks something big is going out down over the Rabbit Festival weekend and Ada just wants to keep ahead of the curve whether it's flattening out or not. To be honest, continued Ada, she does like Karen the Sheep. That's my point argued Spencer, what if it's a honey trap? How is that even possible argued Ada, she's a munter!

8. Other business – none

23. IT'S RABBIT DAY

23rd Lockdown Board Meeting: Sun, 12th April 2020

In Attendance:

Me (Chair)

Spud II (Head of cat dept)

Spencer (Head of bigger dog dept)

Ada (Head of smaller dog dept)

Horny Frank (Head of horny rabbit dept)

Beardy (Head of not so horny rabbit dept)

Apologies - None

Call to order 06:00hrs

1. There were sufficient members for a quorum
2. Minutes of previous meeting approved
3. Business from last meeting: None
4. Statement from the Chair: Happy Easter everyone, hope you all have a reasonable day under these very stressful times. Boris states

that he owes his life to NHS staff, so that's nice. Boris's mate Priti says she's sorry if people feel there were some failings, so that's nice. The Queen stated yesterday, that - death is dark, but light and life are greater, so that's good.

5. Business Updates:
   5.1 Horny Frank: Horny Frank wished everybody a happy Rabbit's Day. Spud asked Horny Frank what this Rabbit Day thing was all about? Horny Frank stated that he had done some serious research into Rabbit's Day and discovered that once upon a time, way before these stressful times, there was a very important German rabbit, called the Judge. His main job was to assess all the young human types and see if they were good or bad. If the young human types were good enough, the Judge brought them, sweeties. Sounds like a load of old baked guff, argued Spud. Ada stated that she thought rabbits were just used as porn logos for pervy human types. Horny Frank replied yes there was that, but only because rabbits are cute, shy, and vivacious. Ada argued that it was all a bit too pervy and twisted for her.
   5.2 Spud: Spud stated that he was sorry for giving Ada what for yesterday. It was just that he was sound asleep under the Chair's crispy dry table, in the shade, away from the hot day's sun. He was having a lovely dream about chasing long tails and all of a sudden Ada turns up for a cuddling session right next to him, probably imagining that he was some cuddly dog type. So he woke up, somewhat startled and let's face it, with tired squinted eyes, Ada does resemble a sizable long tail. So, he gave her 'what for.' Ada stated that she was nowhere near Spud. She just wanted out of the sun for a bit, and without provocation, Spud just went off on one. Plus, Ada stated, she really didn't appreciate the claws coming out, there was no need for that. If she brought her pearly whites out in earnest, added Ada, Spud's hole would know all about it. Spud stated that Ada was once again being a bit aggressive. However, Spud reiterated that he was sorry, but don't come up on his blind side again.
   5.3 Spencer: Spencer stated that he loved those curvy bones the Chair give him and Ada yesterday. He would also appreciate it if Ada didn't steal them, and hide them away; there was plenty for both of them. Nonetheless, very much appreciated. Spencer also stated that he also had never heard of Rabbits Day until now and thought it had more to do with eggs rather than rabbits. Spencer said that from his serious research he

discovered that years ago, way before the stressful times, young human types who were hungry because they had little food, had to go through an *official* period of not eating as well. But before the hungry young human types started their official *not eating period*, they went around the doors and begged for eggs. Not the lovely chocolate type eggs; just the ordinary chicken type eggs. But why the rabbit? asked Spud. Spencer replied that that was only the German types trying to be different by having the young human types judged by a rabbit. In fact, it wasn't even a rabbit; it was a hare.

5.4   Beardy: Beardy thanked Horny Frank for his explanation of Rabbit's Day and stated that Spencer was talking through his kitchen door and wondered if he had a brush-pass with Karen the Sheep. Spencer reassured Beardy that his acquired knowledge did not come from Karen the Sheep nor his kitchen door. Beardy stated that rabbits, are a more modern sophisticated cuniculus type breed, and probably American. The hare is just an overgrown German type throwback, argued Beardy.

5.5   Ada: Ada stated that she was in a very happy place today and not in the slightest bit aggressive, and she is going to avoid all the 'let's love rabbits' weirdo stuff. She still loves her new toy, the black plastic thing, and stated that it must've cost the Chair a fortune, she really does loves it. She's had a busy week protecting the garden area and collecting all that Intel. Today she intends to have a day off, relax, play with her black plastic thing and munch on her Hatchwells special, and if Horny Frank thinks he's coming over to Judge her, she'll Easter bunny his cuniculus ass all the way to the perimeter area.

Other business –none

24. SPENCER'S INFLEXABILITY ISSUE

24th Lockdown Board Meeting: Mon, 13th April 2020

In Attendance:

Me (Chair)

Spud II (Head of cat dept)

Spencer (Head of bigger dog dept)

Ada (Head of smaller dog dept)

Horny Frank (Head of horny rabbit dept)

Beardy (Head of not so horny rabbit dept)

Apologies - None

Call to order 06:00hrs

1. There were sufficient members for a quorum
2. Minutes of previous meeting approved
3. Business from last meeting: None

4. Statement from the Chair: It's a lovely Bright Monday, so that's good. Spain and Italy are easing the lockdowns, so that's good too. Boris stated that the NHS saved his life, so that's nice… again.
5. Business Updates:
    5.1 Horny Frank: Horny Frank asked was there going to be another performance poll this week? The Chair stated no not this week because Ada is such a favourite with the Stakeholders at the moment there'd be no point. Horny Frank argued that that was ridiculous, that he was catching her up in the votes and probably would have caught her, given another day or two more. The Chair stated that that wasn't really true and Horny Frank probably wouldn't have even gotten past Spud, who was in second place. So, you're just going to stop the poll because it doesn't suit anymore? Horny Frank argued. The Chair stated that that was correct, and he will introduce the poll again in a couple of weeks when the Stakeholders have had a chance to re-adjust.
    5.2 Spud: Spud stated that he noticed Spencer was relieving himself in the garden area a lot more nowadays and if it's due to Ada giving off her pleasant smells again, isn't it time that one or both of them were deseeded? The Chair stated that the vet is only open for emergencies, so it's not possible during these stressful times. Then maybe, Spud added, we should consider getting Ada a visit like we did Beardy. Spencer stated that he must object, you can't just invite a strange dog type in to visit Ada when he's here. The Chair indicated that Her Indoors had given it some thought and thinks it's a reasonable idea, and the Chair added that he didn't mind either way. But surely, Spencer continued, he should be allowed to visit her first. After all, he's the one she snuggles up to every night when she's sleepy or during the day when she's knackered coming back from her black ops. Spud stated that Spencer is constantly with her, so how would planning a special visit just for him help in any way? Well, you all persevered with Beardy during Rosie's visit, Spencer added. Spud argued that we know, but it's not quite the same thing now is it? Right, Ada interrupted, she had listened to this guff long enough, if Spencer could've managed it, it would've been sorted by now. He's a great snuggler, and she really does love her snuggles, but his cave hunter won't reach the cave, added Ada.
    5.3 Spencer: Spencer stated that he is absolutely against Ada getting a visit from a strange dog type. He stated that he would like to put it on record that he will not be held

responsible for any damage done to any strange dog type that comes into the garden area to visit Ada. Ada stated that she really understands how Spencer is feeling at the moment. She reiterated that she really loves their snuggles at night and cherishes that feeling of safety, but at the end of the day she needs her potato baked, or she's losing her oven.

5.4 Beardy: Beardy thanked everybody for a wonderful day yesterday; it was just magical, although he did miss the Easter veggie sticks! The Chair apologised, as they weren't essential, he couldn't go and get them. Yes, no Hatchwells special either, stated Ada, was really looking forward to that too. The Chair said that he can only apologise and will make it up when the stressful times are over. But you went out and got Her Indoors that lovely pink chocolate egg, added Ada. I know, but that was a life or death situation, replied the Chair.

5.5 Ada: Ada stated that she was back in black ops mode. There was no sign of Karen the Sheep, so she was probably at up Town, so all quiet on that front. On the matter of her potential visit from a strange type because of Spencer's inflexibility with his cave hunter, she is definitely up for it. Maybe Spencer could get a visit too; he obviously needs a bit of fickey-fick.

6. Other business - The Chair stated that he will consider the fickey-fick concerns within both Dog Departments and put the topic on the agenda for a later meeting and will update the Board regularly on the progress.

25. RLT UPRISING

25th Lockdown Board Meeting: Tues, 14th April 2020

In Attendance:

Me (Chair)

Spud II (Head of cat dept)

Spencer (Head of bigger dog dept)

Ada (Head of smaller dog dept)

Horny Frank (Head of horny rabbit dept)

Beardy (Head of not so horny rabbit dept)

Apologies - None

Call to order 06:00hrs

1. There were sufficient members for a quorum
2. Minutes of previous meeting approved
3. Business from last meeting: None
4. Statement from the Chair: Boris's mate Mr Raab says we're not at the peak yet, so that's not good. Current figures do not cover Care Homes, so that's not good either. The CMO stated that the scale of the virus catastrophe unfolding in Care Homes is dramatically laid bare, so that's not really good.
5. Business Updates:
    5.1 Horny Frank: Horny Frank stated that the fox types were all over the garden area last night and got into a black bag and there was rubbish all over the place. Ada stated that the cat flap wouldn't open, so she couldn't get out to secure the garden area. The Chair apologised and said that it was all his fault, he locked the cat flap by mistake and forgot to put the black bag in the bin. Ada stated that the Chair has to be more careful during these stressful times, especially with regards to the fox types and the long tails. It's bad enough having the fox types around the garden area, but the long tails, well that's a different story, Ada added. They're currently up to no good and in need of some serious controlling. Horny Frank stated that that's going to be tricky, there seems to be more and more of them every week. Ada stated that it's not really tricky, but we do need to think out of the box. The long tails are growing in number yes, therefore slowing that growth is the critical factor in our new potential control strategy. Their rapid growth is affecting our living standards and thus must be halted, Ada added. How? asked Horny Frank. Not sure yet, Ada replied, but we must try and give them something they really need, which in turn slows their reproduction.
    5.2 Spud: Spud stated that the garden area was quiet yesterday, even though it was a lovely sunny day? Usually, the Chair is having a crispy dry time, and everyone is happy, but yesterday there was nothing! The Chair stated that he was still having a crispy dry time in the afternoon, but was inside, listening to his favourite group streaming a 'live gig,' and he was happy. That's all well and good, stated Spud, but it's the lack of activity in the garden area during the day that attracts the visitor types at night. Plus, Spencer and Ada are pains in the hole when they're left on their own for too long. Ada was trying to throw the black plastic thing herself and chase after

it, it was pathetic to watch, and yet Spencer was watching it; doubly pathetic.

5.3 Spencer: Spencer stated that he was very sorry at what he said to Ada yesterday after the Lockdown Board Meeting. Ada was absolutely right for giving him what for after saying what he did. It's just that he was so angry; he couldn't help himself, Spencer added. Ada stated that he was bang out of order and that she had enough to worry about with the long tails in the railway verge area, and he needed to control himself and not let his wee tail waggle his big mouth.

5.4 Ada: Ada stated that she had another brush-pass with Karen the Sheep. She was indeed up Town acting as a babysitter for a couple of high-ranking long tails. Did Karen the Sheep know anything about the attack in the garden area last night? asked Horny Frank. Ada stated that Karen the Sheep had no idea, but she did say probably not long tails. The long tails she was babysitting were two walk-ins who had to be delivered back to The Farm. Ada added that the two long tails were part of a dissident group, calling themselves the RLT. From the Intel Ada received from Karen the Sheep, the RLT has been running contraband up and down the railway verge area in underground tunnels to other garden areas and up Town. What does RLT stand for? asked Beardy. The Real Long Tails replied Ada.

5.5 Beardy: Beardy wanted to know many long tails are in the RLT, and what do they want? No idea of numbers yet but probably small, Ada replied. They want all animal types out of the railway verge area so they can continue their trafficking without interference. So what's happening with Ben the Long Tail? asked Beardy. Ada stated that they weren't sure which side of the fence Ben the Long Tail is sitting on at the moment, but they do know that they are now combating the long tails on two fronts. Not to forget the foxy types, Ada added, they're in on it too in some way, so let's not encourage them.

6. Other business – None

26. RLT ATTACK

26th Lockdown Board Meeting: Wed, 15th April 2020

In Attendance:

Me (Chair)

Spud II (Head of cat dept)

Spencer (Head of bigger dog dept)

Ada (Head of smaller dog dept)

Horny Frank (Head of horny rabbit dept)

Beardy (Head of not so horny rabbit dept)

Apologies - None

Call to order 06:00hrs

1. There were sufficient members for a quorum
2. Minutes of previous meeting approved
3. Business from last meeting: None
4. Statement from the Chair: Boris is negative now, so that's good. Boris's mate Rashi says that - Lockdown will be blamed for the coming economic crash, so that's handy. Boris's mate Rashi also

stated that he wants to be honest about what's coming, so that's good. Mr T stated that the WHO are tremendously useless, and he's not paying them anymore, so that's interesting.

5. Business Updates:

   5.1 Joint update from Horny Frank and Beardy: Horny Frank and Beardy were both playing in the garden area by the old shed during their quality time indoors, only it was outdoors because they weren't brought indoors this time. Anyway, they were nibbling away on the lovely green grass when all of a sudden, out from under the old shed appeared loads of long tails. They had nasty evil intent in their pokey wee eyes. They were vicious-looking, and you could tell that they wanted to give us what for. There were far too many for us to deal with, but we stood our ground, and we were ready for battle. Spud heard our battle cry and came to assist.

   5.2 Spud: Spud stated that he had been relaxing in the kitchen area just by the cat flap, having a mid-afternoon snoozette. When suddenly he heard this almighty scream, then more screams, it sent chills down his spine. He quickly got himself together and headed out through the cat flap, past the Chair's crispy dry table and into the garden area where he saw Horny Frank and Beardy hopping about all over the show, it was surreal. When they eventually calmed down, they said they saw long tails coming out from under the old shed. Spud stated that he went straight to the old shed and secured the area, but he couldn't see anything.

   5.3 Ada: Ada stated that she was also having a mid-afternoon snoozette when first she heard Spud banging through the cat flap, then realised there was a lot of screaming coming from the garden area. She immediately realised that something was amiss and followed behind Spud, out the cat flap, past the Chair's crispy dry table and headed straight to ground zero. As Spud was securing the old shed, Ada headed past the old shed, over to the perimeter area and straight into the railway verge area. There was no sign of the long tails, no doubt they got away, Ada added, down into their sneaky underground tunnels and were probably up Town by then. Ada added that she headed back to the old shed and helped Spud secure the area.

   5.4 Spencer: Spencer stated that the kitchen door was closed as usual, and as he can't fit through the cat flap, he couldn't do anything; but said that there was definitely a racket going on outside in the garden area. Spencer asked both Horny Frank and Beardy how many long tails did they actually see? Horny

Frank said loads, jumping and snarling with their nasty claw-like teeth and devil eyes. Horny Frank stated that he tried to grab one and give it what for, but they were too fast. Beardy indicated that he's not exactly sure how many long tails he saw. Spencer insisted, was it one, two, five, ten? Beardy replied that he didn't actually see any. He was munching away at the lovely green grass when Horny Frank jumped and shouted 'long tails,' 'long tails,' and was looking in the direction of the old shed. They must've legged it when they saw Horny Frank's war dance. So just to be clear Spencer asked, only Horny Frank actually saw the long tails? Ada interrupted, the RLT were spotted, and that's all we need to know to escalate this situation. It's undeniable that the RLT are upping the gameplay now and we need to retaliate asap. Spencer stated he's all for upping the gameplay too, but we need to be sure that this was the dissidents and not just a family of long tails out for their legitimate daily exercise and got lost.

6. Other business – None

27. BIGGER FLAP REQUIRED

27th Lockdown Board Meeting: Thurs, 16th April 2020

In Attendance:

Me (Chair)

Spud II (Head of cat dept)

Spencer (Head of bigger dog dept)

Ada (Head of smaller dog dept)

Horny Frank (Head of horny rabbit dept)

Beardy (Head of not so horny rabbit dept)

Apologies - None

Call to order 06:00hrs

1. There were sufficient members for a quorum
2. Minutes of previous meeting approved
3. Business from last meeting: None
4. Statement from the Chair: Lockdown to continue for a further three weeks, so that's not good. Laura from the BBC seen a letter that stated the testing of care workers is flawed, so that's not good either. Mr T stated that his new drug cured Boris, so that's interesting. Mr Whitty stated that the current way of analysing the data shows that the UK deaths are plateauing, so that's good.
5. Business Updates:
    5.1 Ada: Ada stated that she had hurt her back leg. The Chair said that he had noticed her limping. Ada added that it happened during some serious black ops training yesterday in the railway verge area. Karen the Sheep was instructing us on how to give what for in an underground tunnel situation. We have built some training tunnels, and they are a tight squeeze, and she thinks she damaged herself while trying the head drop manoeuvre. Plus, Ada continued, she also has a bad itch in her ear, and she can't stop scratching it and making it bleed, but Spencer gives it a good lick clean. The Chair stated that he'd have a look at it after the meeting, but in the meantime, stop scratching it. Plus, he added, you're going to have to stop going down into those holes. No can do at the moment, argued Ada, we are living in very stressful times, and we need to be prepared, the RLT are extremely dangerous to our democracy, and they need to be given what for.
    5.2 Spud: Spud stated that he had a brush-pass with the foxy nosed fox and apparently, they want a ceasefire. Spencer said that that's very interesting and asked did they suggest terms? Well, Spud replied, it was just a brief encounter, but from what he gathered, the foxy nosed fox wants to have access to the garden area during the night when moving from different garden areas and stated that in return, they would not touch our bins or even the black bags that are left out by mistake. He also said that we could share Intel. Ada stated that she would have to have a proper brush-pass with the foxy nosed fox to discuss red-lines before we sign any papers. Plus, Ada added, she will test the water with Karen the Sheep later today during her debriefing session about the recent RLT attack. Horny Frank asked shouldn't it be him that gets debriefed by Karen the Sheep regarding the recent RLT attacked, after all,

he was the one involved in it? Ada stated that the debriefing would take place at The Farm and only Ada can go there as it's a highly secure facility and way above Horny Frank's pay grade. Horny Frank stated that he didn't realise he had a pay grade.

5.3 Horny Frank: Horny Frank stated the doors of the hutch are in serious need of a good cleaning. He noticed it the other day but forgot to mention it because of the recent RLT attack. Don't think it's ever been cleaned he added, Her Indoors only does a monthly on the inside of the hutch. The Chair stated that he noticed that too and although it's Her Indoors' chore to maintain the hutch on a monthly basis, she will need help with the doors as she will need access, which means dismantling the hutch from the run. The Chair stated that he would discuss this concern with Her Indoors and keep the Board posted. Horny Frank also added as we're having a ceasefire with the foxy nosed foxes, are Beardy and him safe at night now? Spud stated that that's probably a red-line the foxy nosed foxes couldn't sign up to.

5.4 Beardy: Beardy Stated that he still feels a bit shocked about the recent RLT attack. He added that he had nightmares that the RLT came back and kidnapped him and took him away to their underground tunnels to give him what for. They wore hoods and asked me lots of questions about Karen the Sheep. They were demanding the release of one of their comrades from Ada's detention facility. Ada stated that she released all the long tails as a gesture of goodwill during the Rabbit Festival. Beardy argued that he thought she released the long tails because they were starving to death because she wouldn't feed them. Still a gesture of goodwill though, replied Ada.

5.5 Spencer: Spencer stated that if the Chair still refuses to move on the kitchen door policy could he at least consider getting a bigger flap. The Chair stated that he is concerned that the bigger flaps will encourage bigger visitors! However, he will discuss it with Her Indoors because she's got full control over the flap policy.

6. Other business – None

28. PLAN B

28th Lockdown Board Meeting: Fri, 17th April 2020

In Attendance:

Me (Chair)

Spud II (Head of cat dept)

Spencer (Head of bigger dog dept)

Ada (Head of smaller dog dept)

Horny Frank (Head of horny rabbit dept)

Beardy (Head of not so horny rabbit dept)

Apologies - None

Call to order 06:00hrs

1. There were sufficient members for a quorum
2. Minutes of previous meeting approved
3. Business from last meeting: The Chair stated that he approached Her Indoors regarding the dirty hutch and bigger flap issues brought up at yesterday's meeting. He said that he probably could have planned the discussion somewhat better. Her Indoors had just

got home from work, and he thought it would be better to mention it right away in case he forgets. However, he couldn't get a resolution on the issues, because what she suggested the Chair do with the hutch was logistically impossible. Her Indoors then walked away mumbling something about Dr Dolittle and her wanting me to go off somewhere. Anyway, the upshot of it was, a Plan B is needed for the hutch, and he never got to mention the flaps, so that's still open.

4. Statement from the Chair: Boris's mate Mr Raab stated that if it all goes wrong, it's SAGE's fault, so that's handy. Jeremy from SAGE stated that they didn't follow the WHO's advice because they didn't have the kit, so that's not so good. The NDA stated that their helpline has seen a 25% increase in calls during the lockdown, so that's not good either.

5. Business Updates:
    5.1 Ada: Ada stated that she and Karen the Sheep have decided that it's a good idea for the meet-up with Ada and the foxy nosed foxes to go ahead later today. They have agreed that the collection point should happen in a safe place in the garden area. They also decided that Spud's sleeping place under his favourite bush would be ideal. Spud stated that it's going to stink of mangy foxes now! Ada argued that it couldn't be helped; it's the safest place. Spud indicated that it would probably be better if Spencer did the meet-up at the collection point. Ada is an expert in underground combat, Spud added, but Spencer is more capable in the open if it's a trap and they start dishing out what for. Spencer said that that was definitely the way forward because he could dish out some serious what for.

    5.2 Horny Frank: Horny Frank stated that shouldn't we be worried about the foxy nosed foxes having loads of diseases, even worse than the new human flu. Horny Frank suggested that Spencer could wear some PPE. Spencer asked the Chair, could they get some PPE? The Chair argued that you couldn't get PPE for love nor money, and even when you do get your hands on some, it's way out of date. Horny Frank also thanked the Chair for cleaning the hutch yesterday and added that it looks like a brand-new hutch now.

    5.3 Spencer: Spencer stated that he would definitely attend the meet-up, but only as a floater, Ada should carry out the negotiations, she does that very well and isn't easily fooled, but he'll be ready just in case what for breaks out. Ada agreed and stated that she would give Karen the Sheep the nod for

- the meet-up to go ahead. Ada suggested that a good time would be 10:15hrs, just after the food-run and just before the crispy dry afternoon starts, they don't want to give the foxy nosed foxes the wrong impression.
- 5.4 Spud: Spud stated that Ada had mentioned that Horny Frank was on a different pay scale than her and asked how much money does she get? Ada stated that it's not about money; it's about your RS, which is your reliability status. She, for example, has a TS level, which means she can handle top-secret information. Karen the Sheep has a TS/SCI level, which means she knows a lot more stuff.
- 5.5 Beardy: Beardy stated that money isn't necessary anyway, what would they do with it? Ada stated that Karen the Sheep says money doesn't exist. The Chair said that he must remember that the next time he's at Pets at Home, he'll just tell the salesperson that Karen the Sheep says money doesn't exist and he'll walk out. Beardy argued, yes, but you don't use cash anymore do you, cash is dirty now, you just tap your watch and hey presto, as if by magic! Ada stated that Karen the Sheep is absolutely bang on and that the new human flu was designed to get rid of cash. Spud wanted to know what the China humans had against cash.
6. Other business – None

29. FOXY THE FOXY NOSED FOX

29th 'lockdown' Board meeting: Sat, 18th April 2020

In Attendance:

Me (Chair)

Spud II (Head of cat dept)

Spencer (Head of bigger dog dept)

Ada (Head of smaller dog dept)

Horny Frank (Head of horny rabbit dept)

Beardy (Head of not so horny rabbit dept)

Apologies - None

Call to order 06:00hrs

1. There were sufficient members for a quorum
2. Minutes of previous meeting approved
3. Business from last meeting: The Chair stated that he eventually resumed talks with Her Indoors regarding the flap situation. Her

Indoors stated that the Kitchen Door and the Flap policy are closely linked and are not for changing.
4. End of the Week Statement from the Chair: We have been in lockdown now for four weeks. I want to thank all departments for their cooperation during these stressful times. Our mad but lovable Stakeholders are still happy with our updates, so we will continue until they've had enough of my ramblings. The lockdown continues for a bit longer, but spirits are high, and you'll never walk alone.
5. Statement from the Chair: Chris from NHS Providers warns that PPE supplies will run out in 24hrs, so that's not good. Boris's mate Matt stated that 'he would love to have a magic wand,' so that's good. Unions representing NHS staff are concerned that NHS staff are being asked to reuse PPE and use PPE, which is out of date, so that can't be good.
6. Business Updates:
    6.1 Ada: Ada stated that with regards to the meet-up yesterday with the foxy nosed fox, she and Spencer were at the collection point by Spud's favourite place in the garden area at precisely 10:15hrs as was agreed. One foxy nosed fox turned up 5 mins late. They could tell he wasn't on his own and that others stayed in the shadows. The foxy nosed fox approached gingerly, stated that his name was Foxy, and he turned his hole around for Ada to give it a good sniffin', but she refused. Ada stated that she wasn't going to sniff the hole of a terrorist. Ada introduced herself and Spencer. Foxy the foxy nosed Fox stated that he would like to form a Triple Entente with ourselves and Ben the Long Tail. He stated that he already had an agreement in place with the long tails and it was holding nicely. Ada stated that she would have to speak to Karen the Sheep regarding this. Foxy the foxy nosed Fox added that the Entente wouldn't necessarily involve Karen the Sheep nor anybody else from The Farm. Ada stated that she would have to consult the other Board members in that case. Foxy the foxy nosed Fox also stated that Ada should have a meet-up with Ben the Long Tail as well, as soon as. Ada stated that that would be hard to sell to the Board members after the last RLT attack. Foxy the foxy nosed Fox stated that he's not sure it was the RLT who attacked as they have never claimed responsibility. When he spoke to Ben the Long Tail about the apparent attack, he said 'not in our name.'
    6.2 Spencer: Spencer reiterated that the meet-up went smoothly and Foxy the foxy nosed Fox seemed genuine, but as there was no hole sniffing, it was hard to be sure. Spencer added

that a meet-up with Ben the Long Tail was a good idea, if they're fighting against the RLT also, then that can only be a good thing. He added that he too had concerns about the RLT attack, as Horny Frank was the only one to have seen them. Spencer stated that we should plan a meet-up with Ben the Long Tail, keep our enemies close and all that, but he thinks that Ada could manage that by herself, if not, bring Spud along this time. Spud stated that that's probably not a good idea, he'd give Ben the Long Tail what for without even thinking about it and play with him like Ada plays with her black plastic thing.

6.3 Beardy: Beardy Stated that the more he thinks about the RLT attack, the more he doubts it as well. He really didn't see anything, just Horny Frank jumping up and down screaming; to be honest, that scared the life out of him more. He's starting to believe that Karen the Sheep is trying to get our support for a war against the long tails by introducing false evidence to provoke a reaction, which of course it did. The incident was probably planned to take place around the old shed at a specific time to give the genuine appearance that it was carried out by hostile dissident long tails. Beardy stated that he's starting to wake up.

6.4 Horny Frank: Horny Frank stated that he definitely saw long tails coming out from under the old shed, he'll never forget their beady little eyes glaring at him. He argued that there's no way that attack was staged. If it was planned for maximum effect when he and Beardy were there alone, then how did they know that our quality time indoors was actually taking place outdoors, that was a last-minute change. They definitely came to dish out what for. Beardy asked who made the change to the schedule then, maybe that was part of the plan. The Chair stated that it was Her Indoors that changed the quality time indoors to quality time outdoors because she can. To be honest, argued the Chair, if you think Her Indoors spent time planning a false flag with Karen the Sheep to create tension between us and the long tails, well you're as mad as our Stakeholders. Ada stated that she stands by Karen the Sheep; she wants to bring peace to the railway verge area. Her and The Farm are fighting a war on terror, and that war reached our shores on April 14, 2020. The RLT we face dish out what for in the name of a totalitarian ideology that hates freedom.

6.5 Spud: Spud stated that he's glad the meet-up went well. He also said that he doesn't really trust Karen the Sheep either.

He asked if Ada had actually been to The Farm, and does it even exist? However, in saying all that, he's not sure how he feels about making friends with long tails, it just goes against nature. Spud also stated that whatever agreement we make, we must be able to make our own foreign policy decisions. Ada stated that she had not been to The Farm yet but was planning a visit soon. The Chair said that it's probably time to consult our Stakeholders on the community page again regarding this current predicament we find ourselves in.
7. Other business – None

30. SNARLY KAREN

30th Lockdown Board Meeting: Sun, 19th April 2020

In Attendance:

Me (Chair)

Spud II (Head of cat dept)

Spencer (Head of bigger dog dept)

Ada (Head of smaller dog dept)

Horny Frank (Head of horny rabbit dept)

Beardy (Head of not so horny rabbit dept)

Apologies - None

Call to order 06:00hrs

1. There were sufficient members for a quorum
2. Minutes of previous meeting approved
3. Business from last meeting: None

4. Statement from the Chair: Boris's mate, Prof. Powis stated that the Government was - working incredibly hard to supply PPE to front-line NHS workers, so that's good. The Army delivered PPE to NHS staff one day last month for a photoshoot, which was good. Boris is still sick at number 10, but Captain Tom is healthy at number one, so that's great.
5. Business Updates:
   5.1 Ada: Ada stated that she had a brush-pass with Karen the Sheep in the railway verge area, to discuss the recent meet-up with Foxy the foxy nosed Fox. Karen the Sheep was slightly put out to hear that she wasn't trusted by Foxy the foxy nosed Fox. In fact, she was more than put out; she started making these funny, weird noises and pulling weird snarlish faces. She was angry to be perfectly honest, added Ada, and she's not a pretty sight when she's angry. That crooked look she gives you, those pokey eyes, although great lashes and those yellow earrings do nothing for her! Ada didn't mention the discontentment within the Board; she didn't want to provoke the snarl. Anyway, Ada added that Karen the Sheep calmed down, and decided to take Ada on a visit to The Farm to prove that she is legit. We manoeuvred up the railway verge area in the direction of up Town, past some other garden areas, through very thick thickets. Then we saw them! A sneaky RLT cell in training. They were all over an old busted sofa practising giving each other what for, scrambling out of their underground tunnel, dishing out a bit of what for, then scrambling back down the tunnel. It was precision at its best, incredible to watch.
   5.2 Beardy: Beardy stated that he was glad we're being more cautious with Karen the Sheep and asked when Ada was going for the meet-up with Ben the Long Tail and where? Good question, replied Ada, now that Karen the Sheep isn't involved in the 'talks,' we'll have to open up a back channel ourselves to try and contact Ben the Long Tail. Beardy stated that he could chat to one of the fox type visitors that come into the garden area at night and they could pass a message on to Foxy the foxy nosed Fox, who in turn will arrange the meet-up with Ben the Long Tail. That's a big risk, argued Spencer, if that Intel gets into the wrong paws or claws, or even the odd hoof, that could spell danger.
   5.3 Spencer: Spencer asked Ada what The Farm was like? Ada stated that she never actually got to see The Farm. When they saw the RLT cell training they hid and observed for a while,

they didn't want to expose themselves, because now they know where their training ground is and know the coordinates of a tunnel entrance. So after a while, Ada continued, Karen the Sheep decided that they should head back. Beardy argued that we still don't know if The Farm is real or not. Ada stated that it's obvious it's real, they were on our way there!

5.4 Horny Frank: Horny Frank stated that there's no way he would trust the fox type visitors that comes into the garden area at night. For all we know they could be RLT sympathisers. Horny Frank asked Ada if she'd seen any fox types in the railway verge area, especially near the RLT training cell? Ada stated that she never saw any fox type visitors but could smell that they had been there recently. Horny Frank said that he knew it, they are working together.

5.5 Spud: Spud stated that the collection point for the meet-up should be in the garden area again. Horny Frank argued that the sneaky wee long tails wouldn't come into the garden area especially, during the day when they know Spud is lurking. Ada stated that Horny Frank was right; the collection point should be under the decking in the North East corner on the garden area. It's still in the garden area so safe for us, but also safe for the long tails. Spud asked was Ada really going under the decking area. Ada stated no, there is a broken plank and she can look right down into the under the decking area; therefore, she should be able to see Ben the Long Tail. If Ben the Long Tail jumps out to dish out some what for, Ada continued, she could easily give him what for back, but if she tries to jump down to give him what for because he's been discourteous and acting like a tallywhacker, then she'd get stuck because she's too big and Ben the Long Tail could give her what for all day long.

6. Other business – None

31. THE SNICKERDOODLES

31st Lockdown Board Meeting: Mon, 20th April 2020

In Attendance:

Me (Chair)

Spud II (Head of cat dept)

Spencer (Head of bigger dog dept)

Horny Frank (Head of horny rabbit dept)

Beardy (Head of not so horny rabbit dept; acting Head of smaller dog dept)

Apologies - Ada (Head of smaller dog dept)

Call to order 06:00hrs

1. There were sufficient members for a quorum
2. Minutes of previous meeting approved
3. Business from last meeting: None
4. Statement from the Chair: Harry, formally known as Prince, stated that he is having zero engagement with crappy newspapers, so that's good. Little Mix stated that NHS staff deserve a huge thank

you, ahhh that's nice. Elton rocks the world from his garden, that's nice too. NHS doctors warn they could stop treating patients to protect their own lives as equipment shortages become critical, so that's not so good.

5. Business Updates:

   5.1 Beardy: Beardy stated that he was standing in for Ada as she is off sick today. The Chair stated that Ada is fine and is being well looked after and is on antibiotics. Beardy said that the backchannel worked, and Ada met with Ben the Long Tail yesterday as planned. In Ada's report, she stated that Ben the Long Tail was pleasant and well-spoken. Ben the Long Tail said that The Farm does exist, and Karen the Sheep is their primary agent. He added that The Farm want to control the railway verge area, but the long tails are not sure why yet. The Farm state that they are serving in a peacekeeping capacity, which is very complex and challenging. Ben the Long Tail also stated that he is not the leader of the long tails. The long tails are led by Princess Snickerdoodle who's from a long line of Snickerdoodles reigning over the Principality of Snickerdoodle. However, Ben the Long Tail continued, there are currently two rebel factions that don't like the Snickerdoodles and have therefore become stateless. One is the RLT that you already know about, and the other is the 'Under the Decking Fighting Force' or for short, the UDFF. These two groups hate each other more than they hate the Snickerdoodles. The good point here is that there's no rebel alliance, so they are two separate rebel groups. Princess Snickerdoodle suggested that a friendship is formed for all those who want to keep the railway verge area free and open to all.

   5.2 Spencer: Spencer stated that it now seems a lot worse than he initially thought. He thought they were dealing with a few angry long tails but now Ben the Long Tail is saying that there's a Royal family involved, a Principality for heaven's sake! Spencer stated that he understands The Farm wanting to keep the peace but is not sure how that's possible! Spencer argued that shouldn't we just leave it to Karen the Sheep and The Farm; they can open up their own backchannel with Princess Snickerdoodle and the Principality and let them get on with it? These times are stressful enough without encouraging complex problems that no one will understand. How do we explain this to our most loveable Stakeholders, most of whom should be sectioned already?

5.3 Spud: Spud stated that he wanted to know if Ada got her infection from Ben the Long Tail, or was it from the meet-up with Foxy the foxy nosed Fox, or is it the dreaded human flu? The Chair stated that Ada's ear infection had flared up again, she probably scratched it scrambling down tunnels practising what for, but he's sure she'll be ok after a day's rest. Spud also stated that he agrees with Horny Frank, Princess or not, she's still a long tail, and her weird name doesn't change that fact.

5.4 Horny Frank: Horny Frank stated that we must stand up for peace at all costs. We should jump into bed with Princess Snickerdoodle and keep the railway verge area open to all. Beardy said that in Ada's report, Ben the Long Tail stated that the RLT had comrades captured and imprisoned by Ada at her containment facility just over the perimeter area in the railway verge area side. However, most of the prisoners were non-rebel types. He stated that they are furious at the way they were treated. They stated that their comrades and the non-rebel types were given what for on a daily basis, starved, and then just released with no explanation. Those freed non-rebel types then started the UDFF, and their ranks swelled because of the treatment they had received and the lack of intervention by the RLT and the Snickerdoodles. Beardy stated that the Board should open up an investigation regarding this issue. Spencer said that he's ok with that, as long as it takes a long time to do, and Ada oversees the investigation. In the meantime, Spencer continued, circle the wagons and batten down the hatches.

6. Other business – The Chair stated that an investigation into the concerns raised by Ben the Long Tail from the Snickerdoodle Principality should be opened. However, it will have to wait until the lockdown eases up. Therefore, now that we're dealing with a Principality and over watched by The Farm, our official narrative is as follows: "The Long Tail Gate investigation will open as soon as possible. It is the right thing to do but needs to be done at the right time. Our thoughts go out to all the wee long tails who have been affected by this."

Lockdown Board Meetings 2020

32. THE PECKER KIDS GO MISSING

32nd Lockdown Board Meeting: Tues, 21st April 2020

In Attendance:

Me (Chair)

Spud II (Head of cat dept)

Spencer (Head of bigger dog dept)

Ada (Head of smaller dog dept)

Horny Frank (Head of horny rabbit dept)

Beardy (Head of not so horny rabbit dept)

Apologies - None

Call to order 06:00hrs

1. There were sufficient members for a quorum
2. Minutes of previous meeting approved

3. Business from last meeting: Ada stated that she would like the Long Tail Gate investigation to start sooner rather than later and therefore, it needs to be tabled today.
4. Statement from the Chair: Lockdown in Europe and America gently lifts, so that's good. Oil is currently free, so that's good too. Harry, formally known as Prince, and his missus were spotted, wearing blue bandanas as face masks, delivering Angel Food to the critically ill, so that's great.
5. Business Updates:
    5.1 Beardy: Beardy stated that he's happy for the Long Tail Gate investigation to get started as soon as. If we've nothing to hide, we've nothing to worry about, he added. Spencer agreed, let's get it done and dusted, we don't want fake news coming from The Farm or used by the RLT or the UDFF as an excuse for lamenting and poem writing. Ada thanked Beardy and Spencer and added that we need to keep this narrative tight. Beardy stated that if nothing happened, then Ada shouldn't get too stressed out over it. Spud stated that he couldn't see The Farm getting all worked up over a few skinny long tails yammering on about missing a few meals. Granted, Spud continued, Princess Snickerdoodle and her mate Ben the Long Tail might have a few issues, but again, who's going to get worked up about it? Ada stated that during these stressful times you don't really know what's going on out there, and why all of a sudden is the railway verge area so important? While we're in the dark, we need to keep it tight.
    5.2 Spencer: Spencer stated that while he was patrolling the perimeter area between the garden area and the railway verge area, he had a brush-pass with a pecker. Horny Frank asked if Spencer give the pecker what for. Spencer stated that he was ready to give the pecker what for when he thought maybe the pecker's just lost, and that in light of the Long Tail Gate investigation hanging over us, he thought he would ask questions first. He's glad he did, he added, because the pecker was only looking for his kids. The pecker stated that he's from up near Elsewhere, and the kids were playing in their garden area, and he went off pecking for a minute or two and the next thing he knew, they were gone. He thought they had just strayed off over into the railway verge area and couldn't get back. So, the pecker had been checking all the other garden areas along the railway verge area just searching for his kids.
    5.3 Spud: Spud stated that that's pretty annoying, pecker kids are quite tasty. Spencer argued that these aren't the times to be

self-seeking and infernal and added that in light of the potential new friendship suggested by Princess Snickerdoodle from the Principality of Snickerdoodle, he told the pecker that we the Board would help him find his pecker kids. Yes, Spud argued, but for all we know the long tails could have the pecker kids held up underground somewhere, maybe for some sort of leverage later on for whatever they're planning.

    5.4 Ada: Ada stated that that's a great idea, it would be a great PR exercise if we helped find the pecker kids. She said that she would plan a search-and-recovery mission immediately and head out this morning after the food-run and before crispy dry afternoon starts. Ada asked the Chair could he do the food-run early this morning in light of these recent developments? The Chair said no. Ok fair enough, replied Ada, they'll head out at 10:15hrs. Ada suggested that he and Spud should join with the pecker and go deep into the railway verge area. We could start with a brush-pass with Karen the Sheep to see if she's heard anything, then head West towards Elsewhere and back before dark.

    5.5 Horny Frank: Horny Frank stated that he appreciates Spud's theories regarding the pecker kids, but maybe they should involve Foxy the foxy nosed Fox and Ben the Long Tail? Ada argued that that's not a good idea at the moment. The pecker kids have probably just wandered off and got lost, and it should be easy to find them. When we do find them, we can publicise the doo-doo out of it, make a wee video of us dancing, and record a song with Little Mix. Then, when everybody is singing our praises and flying rainbow flags, we'll quietly release the Long Tail Gate Report. Beardy asked Ada, with all these new developments, when would she find the time to investigate, write and then publish the Long Tail Gate Report? Ada stated that it's completed already, and all set to go. That's excellent, replied Horny Frank, does the pecker have a name? Yes, he's called Gregory, replied Spencer.

6. Other business – None

33. THE PASSPORT

33rd Lockdown Board Meeting: Wed, 22nd April 2020

In Attendance:

Me (Chair)

Spud II (Head of cat dept)

Spencer (Head of bigger dog dept)

Ada (Head of smaller dog dept)

Horny Frank (Head of horny rabbit dept)

Beardy (Head of not so horny rabbit dept)

Apologies - None

Call to order 06:00hrs

1. There were sufficient members for a quorum
2. Minutes of previous meeting approved
3. Business from last meeting: None

4. Statement from the Chair: ONS stated that deaths increased by 130% above a 20-year average last week, so that's not good. ONS also stated that 66% of the increase was not due to the virus, that's not so good either. Sir Jeremy from Welcome stated that we've passed the peak of the virus, so that is good.
5. Business Updates:
    5.1 Ada: Ada stated that the search and rescue mission team, consisting of herself, Spud and Gregory the Pecker, assembled at the perimeter area between the garden area and the railway verge area at the agreed time of 10:15hrs yesterday. The Chair was late with the food-run again, so we had to go without din-dins. The Chair apologised, he stated that he was just running a bit late. They went over into the railway verge area, continued Ada, and the first port of call was a brush-pass with Karen the Sheep. Arriving at Karen the Sheep's safe house at the old outhouse, Karen the Sheep seemed a bit more sheepish than usual. Karen the Sheep informed Ada and the team, that she was on the run from The Farm and seeking asylum. Karen the Sheep asked if she could be harboured in our garden area and apply for asylum there.
    5.2 Spencer: Spencer asked Ada why Karen the Sheep was on the run from The Farm. Ada stated that she had lots of documents laying out top-secret plans and missions from The Farm. That's very interesting; continued Spencer, is she going to let us have a butchers? Only if she gets her asylum application granted in our garden area. Spencer asked the Chair if Karen the Sheep could stay in our garden area for a while as a refugee and apply for asylum? The Chair said no way Jose. Spud agreed with the Chair; we don't want to get involved in any Sheepileak stand-off with The Farm. Beardy stated that it was illegal not to let her stay as an asylee while her application gets investigated. The Chair said that he doesn't care; he doesn't want a sheep in his garden area.
    5.3 Spud: Spud stated that apart from the interesting Sheepileak stuff, Karen the Sheep had nothing to offer us regarding the missing pecker kids, although she did hint that pecker kids were a highly sought-after delicacy up Town, which was understandable. So, we headed out West in the direction of Elsewhere. It was reasonably plain sailing, right up to the garden area where the pecker kids were last seen. Gregory the Pecker went into his garden area to visit missus Pecker while Spud and Ada stayed in the railway verge area and searched for clues of any kind. They found an incredible machine which

they searched but nothing of any significance. However, they did find a few holes, some small, some larger which definitely looked like tunnel entrances.

5.4 Beardy: Beardy asked if they found any clues? Ada said yes, they got very lucky, near one of the small tunnel entrances they found a passport. Excellent stuff, who did it belong to, asked Beardy? It belonged to a long tail called Roger from the Principality of Snickerdoodle. No way stated Beardy, that's a turn up for the books, and you found it at an entrance to a tunnel! It was the long tails all along. Well, said Spencer, it's too early to jump to conclusions, we need to find this Roger the Long Tail and see what side of the fence his bread is buttered on first. It's vital that we see the documents that Karen the Sheep has, Beardy continued, they might contain a clue. All's well and good, argued Spencer, but the Chair said that he doesn't want a Sheep in his garden area! Beardy asked the Chair to reconsider his 'no Sheep in the garden area' policy, given the implications of the passport discovery. The Chair stated that he'd consult Her Indoors but added, don't hold your breath.

5.5 Horny Frank: Horny Frank stated that it is going to be very hard for the long tails to wriggle their way out of this one. What was a long tail from Snickerdoodle doing so far West, on his way to Elsewhere maybe? Does that tunnel head back East toward Snickerdoodle and perhaps even on to The Farm, or worse up Town? What business would Roger the Long Tail have in Elsewhere? What did Gregory the Pecker think? asked Horny Frank. Well, said Spud, when he got back to us, he looked pretty down in the beak. Missus Pecker was very upset that her pecker kids weren't found yet, and Gregory the Pecker said that peckers go missing all the time, they get used to it, their wee pecker eggs go missing every day, and they've no idea where or why. Missus Pecker lost a half a dozen of pecker eggs the other day, she had just laid them, then they went for a peck and a cluck, came back and they were gone! But pecker kids, that's different. Now she's just sitting there staring towards the railway verge area, not interested in a cluck whatsoever. He offered her a quick cluck before he left again, but she told him to go cluck himself, it's very heart-breaking, he continued, no pecker likes to cluck on their own. Spud stated that Ada told Gregory the Pecker not to worry, that we will get the pecker kids back for missus Pecker and we won't stop for one second until they're back safe. Did you continue

searching right away then? asked Horny Frank. Nah, we stopped for a rest first, replied Ada.
6. Other business – None

34. THE RETURN OF THE BIG FOREIGN BIRD

34th Lockdown Board Meeting: Thurs, 23rd April 2020

In Attendance:

Me (Chair)

Spud II (Head of cat dept)

Spencer (Head of bigger dog dept)

Ada (Head of smaller dog dept)

Horny Frank (Head of horny rabbit dept)

Beardy (Head of not so horny rabbit dept)

Apologies - None

Call to order 06:00hrs

1. There were sufficient members for a quorum
2. Minutes of previous meeting approved

3. Business from last meeting: The Chair stated that he consulted Her Indoors regarding the relaxing of the current 'no Sheep in the garden area' policy, and she said never.
4. Statement from the Chair: Boris's mate Matt states that the vaccine trials start today, so that's good. ONS stated that 10% of all the virus deaths happen in Care Homes, so that's still not good. Prince Louis made a rainbow poster, so that's nice.
5. Business Updates:
    5.1 Spencer: Spencer stated that we had a visit from the Big Foreign Bird yesterday which turned out to be very helpful. She told us she's from up Town and she heard about the missing pecker kids and wanted to help. She wanted a brush-pass with Gregory the Pecker, so we arranged it immediately in the garden area. The Big Foreign Bird asked Gregory the Pecker if he'd seen the Sheepileak documents Karen the Sheep stole from The Farm. Gregory the Pecker told her we hadn't because of the current 'no Sheep in the garden area' policy, but he believes that the peckers garden area will grant Karen the Sheep asylum so hopefully, he'll get to see them then. The Big Foreign Bird stated that Karen the Sheep must go there as soon as, get her asylum sorted, which means Gregory the Pecker can get a butchers of the Sheepileak documents and report back. The Big Foreign Bird also asked if we had come across the incredible machine during our search-and-recovery mission in the railway verge area? Gregory the Pecker stated that Spud and Ada searched the incredible machine but found nothing of any use.
    5.2 Ada: Ada stated that she had communications from Ben the Long Tail and Foxy the foxy nosed Fox. Ben the Long Tail asked to see the passport that was recovered. He stated that he didn't know a Roger the Long Tail but will look into it. Princess Snickerdoodle sent her best wishes to the Pecker family and vowed that she would help in whatever way she can. Foxy the foxy nosed Fox stated that although there's a bit of history between them and the peckers, he actually likes peckers, although he couldn't eat a whole one. Nobody likes to see missing pecker kids though. Foxy the foxy nosed Fox added, we'll keep a close ear to the ground and feedback any appropriate Intel but insisted that we continue with Princesses Snickerdoodles friendship agreement.
    5.3 Spud: Spud stated that we the Board, need to see the Sheepileak documents too. One of us should go back to the peckers garden area with Karen the Sheep and the Big Foreign

Bird and have a butchers. Plus, Spud added, we should also give the incredible machine a once over again, just in case we missed something the last time. Spud also said that we have to search the railway verge area to the East, toward The Farm and up Town, we can't ease up now. He thinks those RLT tunnels are linked to the missing pecker kids somehow.

5.4 Beardy: Beardy stated that he agreed with Spud, we have to look East as well. It's strange, after all this time the Big Foreign Bird returns, telling us to go back West and search harder! Spud stated that it's just weird that Karen the Sheep steals the Sheepileak documents and legs it, and then the pecker kids go missing, and now the Big Foreign Bird returns wanting to help save the day. Now to top it all, agreed Beardy, Gregory the Pecker and the Big Foreign Bird are best friends forever! It's as fishy as a fishy thing on fish day, replied Spud. So, what's the plan then? asked Ada. You go with Gregory the Pecker back to the peckers garden area, replied Spud, Ada should keep an eye on the Big Foreign Bird, and have another search around the incredible machine just in case. He'll head East along the railway verge area and get a closer look at those RLT tunnels near the busted sofa. Spencer stated that he'd patrol the perimeter area between the garden area and the railway verge area until they get back and Beardy and Horny Frank can patrol the garden area. Excellent, said Beardy, that's sweet as, meet at the usual time at 10:15hrs before heading off? As good a time as any replied Ada, let's do this.

5.5 Horny Frank: Horny Frank stated that the Chair can guard the crispy dry table, which always gets a seriously good guarding every afternoon starting at 10:30hrs; and no doubt will begin cooking meat outside again as it looks like it's going to be another hot one. The Chair stated that that's precisely his plan and added that he's glad the Board have the peckers in hand, but could they not keep inviting all the avian types into the garden area, especially when he's cooking chicken, doesn't seem right somehow. Horny Frank stated that it's the smell, he wasn't fond of the smell of the avian types at the best of times, but they're definitely smelling a wee bit smellier at the moment. Spud stated that he knows exactly what Horny Frank means, this 'oh where's my wee pecker kids gone' malarkey could be a sneaky wee trick. No way, argued Ada, the peckers are definitely distraught about their missing peckers, you really can tell when someone loses their pecker.

6. Other Business – None

35. TUCKER THE SHEEPDOG

35th Lockdown Board Meeting: Fri, 24th April 2020

In Attendance:

Me (Chair)

Spud II (Head of cat dept)

Spencer (Head of bigger dog dept)

Ada (Head of smaller dog dept)

Horny Frank (Head of horny rabbit dept)

Beardy (Head of not so horny rabbit dept)

Apologies - None

Call to order 06:00hrs

1. There were sufficient members for a quorum
2. Minutes of previous meeting approved
3. Business from last meeting: None

4. Statement from the Chair: Nuclear submarine crew caught enjoying themselves, so that's not good. Malin from Love Island stated that becoming a carer during this pandemic was beautiful, so that's good. B&Q has opened up again, so that's really good.
5. Business Updates:
    5.1 Spud: Spud stated that he left the garden area yesterday at 10:15hrs as agreed and headed over the perimeter area into the railway verge area and headed East in the up Town direction. He passed through the thick thickets until he reached the busted sofa area by the RLT training ground. The area was all clear of the RLT, so he searched the tunnel entrances and found nothing of any interest, just a strong smell of long tails. It was very quiet, although it was a hot day and the RLT could all be just resting, out of the midday sun. Spud added that he had a little snoozette on the busted sofa for a few minutes and then headed back. However, he did notice a blue furry creature not far from the perimeter area, hiding and lurking in the thick thickets, nasty looking thing. He stated that he was too hungry to go and give it what for. Ada argued that Spud should have given it what for, can't take any chances nowadays. Ada added that as soon as this meeting is over, she's going straight out on a special op into the railway verge area to hunt down that blue furry creature and give it what for and arrest it for questioning.
    5.2 Beardy: Beardy stated that he and Horny Frank had a visit from a long tail while they were patrolling the garden area. The long tail appeared from under the old shed area and made it quite clear that he only wanted to talk and had not come to engage us in a what for session, which is just as well because when Horny Frank stopped hopping up and down, we would have seen him off good and proper like. Anyway, just when you think this saga couldn't get any more complicated, the sneaky long tail stated that he represented The Farm and was not from Snickerdoodle. And there's more; he was only asking after the stolen Sheepileak documents and Roger the Long Tail's passport! He stated that if he could have all the stolen Sheepileak documents and the passport back in one piece, he would give us information to help in the recovery of the missing pecker kids.
    5.3 Spencer: Spencer stated that that was all very interesting indeed, he personally would had detained the long tail if he had have seen him, he's obviously in bed with Roger the Long Tail, and they definitely have the answers. These stolen

Sheepileak documents are obviously very important to The Farm, and how would The Farm know details regarding the missing pecker kids if they weren't involved? The plot definitely thickens. The long tail also asked after the Big Foreign Bird and said don't let her get her claws on those stolen Sheepileak documents. Spud stated that it's all a bit late now, Karen the Sheep is at the peckers garden with the Big Foreign Bird having a good old butchers as we speak. So we can kiss goodbye to the pecker kids, added Spud.

5.4 Horny Frank: Horny Frank stated that Ada should be careful with the blue furry creature, especially if you're going to detain it, we're in this predicament with the UDFF because of Ada's detainment skills! That's all nonsense, argued Ada, the Long Tail Gate investigation report will prove that. Horny Frank asked Spud to describe the blue furry creature. Well, replied Spud, it was blue, it was furry, and it looked like a creature. Was it a long tail asked? asked Horny Frank. Well it did have a long tail but slightly bigger than a long tail type, and it was blue, so unless it's a big long tail with a rinse, he doesn't think so, replied Spud. Anyway, he's sure the blue furry creature won't help us save the pecker kids now!

5.5 Ada: Ada stated that she should have her say before they all start wallowing in their own doo-doo. When she headed off over the perimeter area between the garden area and railway verge area at 10:15hrs and headed West in the Elsewhere direction with Gregory the Pecker, Karen the Sheep and the Big Foreign Bird, she became more and more concerned about Karen the Sheep. She looked so worried and concerned and was keeping her distance from the Big Foreign Bird. At first, Ada thought she was socially distancing because of the human flu, but then realised that she was deliberately trying to avoid any conversation with the Big Foreign Bird. When they reached the peckers garden area, Gregory the Pecker and the Big Foreign Bird were having a private chat and Ada took Karen the Sheep down toward the incredible machine, she had to search the incredible machine again anyway, and it would give Karen the Sheep a wee break for a moment, kill two birds with one stone. After a while, added Ada, Gregory the Pecker came and retrieved Karen the Sheep and headed toward the peckers garden area to start the asylum application. Then, all of a sudden out of the blue, a sheepdog type wearing a blue high vis jacket, with the words 'Tucker the Sheepdog' clearly printed on it, turned up and started to round-up Karen the Sheep saying, 'back to The Farm with you,' and off they went, and the Big Foreign Bird did a disappearing act as well! Well reiterated Spud, that's that then, we can kiss goodbye to the pecker kids. Hold your horses, stated Ada, while she was looking after Karen the Sheep at the incredible machine, she stole the stolen Sheepileak documents.

6. Other business – None

36. THE DEATH OF THE BLUE FURRY CREATURE

36th Lockdown Board Meeting: Sat, 25th April 2020

In Attendance:

Me (Chair)

Spud II (Head of cat dept)

Spencer (Head of bigger dog dept)

Ada (Head of smaller dog dept)

Horny Frank (Head of horny rabbit dept)

Beardy (Head of not so horny rabbit dept)

Apologies - None

Call to order 06:00hrs

1. There were sufficient members for a quorum
2. Minutes of previous meeting approved
3. Business from last meeting: None

4. End of the Week Statement from the Chair: We have been in lockdown now for five weeks. I want to thank all departments for their cooperation during these stressful times. Our mad but lovable Stakeholders are still happy, albeit somewhat confused with our updates, or what some might say, the ramblings of a headcase. So, we will continue for a bit longer. The lockdown continues, although it seems we are - in the peak, according to the Chief Medical Officer. Football could be back on in a couple of weeks too.
5. Statement from the Chair: BHF's Dr Sonya states that since Lockdown, there's been a fall of 50% in general medical emergencies attending A&E, so that's not good. Boris's best mate Dominic is helping SAGE make decisions, so that's different. Boris's other mate, Mr Tugendhat aims to - promote debate and fresh thinking, with regards to China, so that's interesting.
6. Business Updates:
    6.1 Ada: Ada stated that she went on the special ops into the railway verge area in the hunt for the blue furry creature right after the meeting yesterday. It was still exactly where Spud had spotted it the day before. She sneaked up and pounced on it and proceeded to give it a serious what for. It didn't react much, which she thought was strange, in fact it didn't react at all! She then realised that the blue furry creature was dead! She didn't want to leave it there, especially with her paw prints all over it. So she brought it back to the garden area for further investigations and to give it a proper burial, in lime. Spud thought it looked a bit still and lifeless the other day, he added. Then what happened? asked Beardy. Well, the Chair saw it and took it off her and stated that it belonged to Her Indoors, she had lost it and couldn't find it anywhere. Didn't know Her Indoors owned a blue furry creature, albeit a dead one, said Beardy, was she broken-hearted? No idea replied Ada.
    6.2 Spud: Spud asked what we intended to do with the stolen stolen Sheepileak documents? Ada stated that the documents are sealed with wax. Let's crack it open, said Horny Frank, and have a butchers, see what all the fuss was about. Hang on a minute, argued Spencer, let's think about this carefully. The stolen stolen Sheepileak documents are obviously very important to The Farm and they have the information that will help us get the pecker kids back home safely. Spencer suggested that we don't have a butchers, and that we keep the wax seal secure. That way if we don't see anything, then we don't know anything; therefore The Farm should be content,

which will, in turn, give us better leverage. That's pretty lame, argued Horny Frank, the suspense was killing him. Spencer's right, agreed Beardy, the suspense is killing us all, but we need to think about the pecker kids first, probably all in code anyway, plus, Beardy added, there's a meet-up request for an exchange.

6.3 Beardy: Beardy stated that he had another meet up with the long tail from The Farm. He turned up at the hutch last night. They are very keen to retrieve the stolen stolen Sheepileak documents as soon as possible. The long tail stated that he knows who has the pecker kids, and The Farm will use their widespread influence to organise the return of the pecker kids in exchange for the stolen stolen Sheepileak documents. They probably have the pecker kids anyway replied, Horny Frank, what did they want with them in the first place? It wasn't for this exchange that's for sure; this is just an inconvenience for them- that we created. Still stated Spencer, let's give them what they want, get the pecker kids back home safely to Gregory and missus Pecker and we can re-group afterwards.

6.4 Horny Frank: Horny Frank reluctantly agreed and stated that that was probably the logical way forward. So what's the plan stan, asked Horny Frank. Well replied Beardy, the long tail said that the exchange should take place today at 10:00hrs at the incredible machine near the peckers garden area. That's the food-run time, Spud replied! What's the chances? Spud asked the Chair. None replied the Chair. Fair enough conceded Spud; we can grab something on the way, although he does hate going on hostage exchanges without din-dins first

6.5 Spencer: Spencer stated, no need to worry about the food-run because he should go alone and make the exchange, just in case Tucker the Sheepdog makes an appearance again. Let him try and round him up, stated Spencer; he'll bury his pearlies into his sheepdog hole. Ada asked if Spencer needed any backup, she fancies a bit of hole chewing, after all, she's on a roll from killing the dead blue furry creature. Better not replied Spencer, you all need to stay put in the garden area in case this is all an elaborate trap.

7. Other business – None

37. THE HOSTAGE EXCHANGE

37th Lockdown Board Meeting: Sun, 26th April 2020

In Attendance:

Me (Chair)

Spud II (Head of cat dept)

Spencer (Head of bigger dog dept)

Ada (Head of smaller dog dept)

Horny Frank (Head of horny rabbit dept)

Beardy (Head of not so horny rabbit dept)

Apologies - None

Call to order 06:00hrs

1. There were sufficient members for a quorum
2. Minutes of previous meeting approved
3. Business from last meeting: None

4. Statement from the Chair: The Army is now testing essential workers, so that's good. Crime is down by 25% in Scotland, so that's good too. Cemeteries are now open in Belfast, so that's excellent, I think!
5. Business Updates:
    5.1 Spencer: Spencer stated that he was up early yesterday morning as Ada woke him up screaming and shouting and running in and out of the cat flap, he knew it was early because it was just getting light outside. Then the Chair came into the kitchen area wondering what all the fuss was about, unlocked the kitchen door and went out into the garden area, *and* he had to get up and follow him out because that's his job. As it happens, it was Her Nextdoor, but that's a story for another time. As he was now up, he had a run around the garden area a few times for a bit of a warm-up exercise and tried to get his head focused for the day's big event. At around 08:30hrs the Board assembled for an extraordinary short meeting, just to make sure they were all still happy with the plan and they all agreed they were, so it was full steam ahead.
    5.2 Ada: Ada stated that she hadn't realised it was Her Nextdoor, and that's early to be up and about for any normal human, type, except for the Chair, he's always up at that time! The Chair stated that Her Nextdoor was just going for an early morning run and she wanted to go through her garden area so she didn't wake the rest of her house up. That's ok, but she woke our whole house up in the process, argued Spencer. Not really, the Chair stated, it was 05:00hrs and he was already up and Her Indoors never heard a thing, so all was well, no train crash. If there's a noise in the garden area at that time of the morning, Ada stated, she will be there screaming and shouting every time, it's her job as well! No arguments there, the Chair replied. Ada also said that she published the Long Tail Gate investigation report last night.
    5.3 Spud: Anyway, interrupted Spud, can we get back to Spencer's story. Spencer thanked Spud and stated that he went over the perimeter area between the garden area and the railway verge area and headed West towards Elsewhere. Were there any signs of anybody else around and about at this stage? asked Spud. No, replied Spencer, all as quiet as, and even when he got to near the peckers garden area, he hung back a bit and waited, still no signs of anything. Not even the peckers? asked Spud. No, not even the peckers, but then they didn't know the exchange was taking place to be fair. He then went a bit closer

and could now eyeball the incredible machine, still nothing there. At this stage he was sure it was past the agreed time of 10:00hrs.

5.4 Beardy: Beardy asked did Spencer thinking the peckers were involved in some way at that stage? Not really, said Spencer, he was too busy concentrating on the incredible machine, he just sat there in the undergrowth and watched. They were probably doing the same thing at the time. He decided to make a move, so he stood up and walked out a bit, and then he saw it, the head off the Big Foreign Bird in the incredible machine. Was she dead? asked Beardy. No, her head was still attached to her body; he could only see her head from where he was. Spencer then stated that he walked out toward the incredible machine, and the Big Foreign Bird showed herself in all her glory. She was on her own from what he could see. Horny Frank asked if the Big Foreign Bird said anything? She asked if he had the stolen stolen Sheepileak documents, Spencer said he did, and held them in the air and stated that the seal was still intact. Spencer asked if she had the pecker kids, she stated that she did, and they appeared on the incredible machine. The Big Foreign Bird asked me to leave the stolen stolen Sheepileak documents on the ground, and for Spencer to walk toward the incredible machine to collect the pecker kids, so he started walking. They passed each other at the halfway mark, then she ran, grabbed the stolen stolen Sheepileak documents and disappeared into the undergrowth. As he got to the incredible machine Spencer added, Gregory the Pecker turned up wondering what all the fuss was about and was then overjoyed to see the pecker kids. Then, missus Pecker turned up clucking like she's never clucked before, then soon the whole place was crawling with peckers, never seen such a clutch of clucking peckers.

5.5 Horny Frank: Horny Frank stated that Her Nextdoor woke him up as well and he hadn't long been asleep, it was a right racket to be fair. The Chair should pay her a visit and sort her out, Horny Frank added. The Chair stated that he was not paying Her Nextdoor a visit. Then invite her over in the afternoon, said Ada, and give her a crispy dry one.

6. Other business – None

38. THE FARM

38th Lockdown Board Meeting: Mon, 27th April 2020

In Attendance:

Me (Chair)

Spud II (Head of cat dept)

Spencer (Head of bigger dog dept)

Ada (Head of smaller dog dept)

Horny Frank (Head of horny rabbit dept)

Beardy (Head of not so horny rabbit dept)

Apologies - None

Call to order 06:00hrs

1. There were sufficient members for a quorum
2. Minutes of previous meeting approved
3. Business from last meeting: None
4. Statement from the Chair: Boris is back and raring to go, so that's good. NDA helpline calls are now up by 50% during this lockdown, so that's still increasing. Deputy CMO, Prof. Jonathan

stated that the - weekend figures show that the UK has passed the peak of the virus, so that's good. The figures are down every weekend, it's a weekend thing, so that's interesting.

5. Business Updates:
   5.1 Spencer: Spencer stated that all was quiet this morning, he got a good sleep in, no racket from Ada nor Her Nextdoor, which was a lovely start to a Sunday. Beardy asked Spencer was there a Him Nextdoor? Spencer replied that he had no idea. Horny Frank said that he never knew there even was a Nextdoor. Ada stated that she thinks there is a Him Nextdoor, but never actually seen him; he never ventures out into their garden area. There is a Nextdoor's Kid though, Ada added. How do you know? asked Spencer. We've played together, replied Ada, Nextdoor's Kid gives her loads and loads of cuddles, she's a real cuddler. You've been in Her Nextdoor's garden area? asked Spencer. Yes, loads of times, replied Ada, she has wee secret tunnel, which leads right into Her Nextdoor's onion patch. Bet they feed you too? asked Beardy. Well when you're this cute, it's hard not to, replied Ada.
   5.2 Ada: Ada stated that she and Spud found The Farm. What do you mean you found The Farm? interrupted Spencer. We found The Farm, replied Ada! Spencer argued that he doesn't remember that 'operation' being planned and agreed by the Board! Her and Spud, Ada continued, were just doing a wee patrol in our local vicinity, in the railway verge area. We checked out the old outhouse where Karen the Sheep used to hide, just to see if there was anything of interest left there. There wasn't.
   5.3 Spud: Spud stated that we then just thought about Karen the Sheep being held prisoner at The Farm and started to wonder where it was. Then the next thing we knew we were heading East along the railway verge towards up Town. We passed through the thick thickets, past the busted sofa and the entrances to the long tail tunnels, all was clear. Continued through more thickety thickets and then we saw it, The Farm. What was it like? asked Beardy. It was like a farm, replied Spud, a big field with sheep types, including Karen the Sheep in it. Karen the Sheep did look miserable, more miserable than usual, Ada added, all sad and bloated. That'll be all that processed crap they feed them, drains their energy, keeps them sleepy so they won't think about stealing secret information and escaping, added Beardy.

5.4 Beardy: Beardy stated that on a different note, Her Indoors appeared yesterday at the hutch. It wasn't monthly time for the hutch, so he was surprised to see her. She did have a face on her though! Apologies for that interrupted the Chair. The Chair stated that he and Her Indoors had words that morning. She came into the kitchen area when she just got up, she was still half a sleep and she so isn't a morning person, plus she was up a bit earlier than she wanted if you're getting the picture. Anyway, the first thing she said was, 'the kitchen smells of dogs.' Now, the Chair continued, he had a dilemma. Her statement, although not a question, demanded a response, he knew that. However, he knew from experience, it was very unlikely that any response he gives will not necessarily neutralise the newly formed atmosphere. But he had to try, because not responding could well make it worse! Now he could've said, 'fancy a coffee and a bit of toast luv?' that would've easily eased the tension, but unfortunately, he thought of that afterwards during his crispy dry time, that's when he gets all his better ideas. What he actually said was, 'that'll be the dogs then.' The face on it!

5.5 Horny Frank: Horny Frank stated that he was happy that Spud and Ada took an executive decision and hunted down The Farm. It was boring here yesterday now that the pecker kids' saga is over. That's a good thing, said Spencer, it was getting mad here for a while. He appreciates that, argued Horny Frank, but who's going to read our updates when it's just us lazing around doing nothing? 'Today Spencer had snooze…Today Spud had a snooze too… Today Ada played with some stupid plastic thing…Today Horny Frank and Beardy dreamt of Rosie and the Chair had a crispy dry one.' You see, added Horny Frank, very very boring. So let's investigate The Farm, help Karen the Sheep out of her misery and start a new saga.

5.6 Other business – None.

39. THE BLACK CAT

39th Lockdown Board Meeting: Tues, 28th April 2020

In Attendance:

Me (Chair)

Spud II (Head of cat dept)

Spencer (Head of bigger dog dept)

Ada (Head of smaller dog dept)

Horny Frank (Head of horny rabbit dept)

Beardy (Head of not so horny rabbit dept)

Apologies - None

Call to order 06:00hrs

1. There were sufficient members for a quorum
2. Minutes of previous meeting approved
3. Business from last meeting: None

4. Statement from the Chair: Boris stated that he has shielded the NHS from the virus, and it is now safe, so that's good. NHS hospitals are starting to manage the millions of cancelled operations now, so that's good too. Boris stated that - it's time to fire up the engines, so that's great.
5. Business Updates:
    5.1 Ada: Ada stated that she went on a reconnaissance mission in the railway verge area yesterday. Not a deep and meaningful one, just a quick looksy. She's glad she did though because she had a brush-pass with a black cat. Who's the black cat? asked Beardy. Well, continued Ada, the black cat was up a tree, sitting on a branch, just lurking. He said he was from up Town and was given the job to keep the long tails out of the railway verge area. Ada asked him who gave him the job and he said the People from up Town. The Chair interrupted; before he forgets he stated that Her Nextdoor complained that Ada is stealing the Nextdoor Kid's toys from their garden area and bringing them into our garden area and breaking them up, especially her favourite ball. There's no point in denying it because the Chair saw her. She wasn't going to deny it, argued Ada, she was given those toys, especially the ball, as a present. When she visits Her Nextdoor's garden area, Nextdoor's Kid gives her a few cuddles and then throws the toys and says, 'there Asda, there Asda,' she calls her Asda, Ada added.
    5.2 Spud: Spud asked, is that because Ada doesn't settle for less? No idea replied Ada, she doesn't really speak much to be honest. Anyway, interrupted the Chair again, Her Nextdoor had a serious word in his shell-like, and he had to replace the toys. Her Nextdoor is playing up all of a sudden, stated Spud. Only because of Ada's stealing, so it must stop, the Chair stated, and he has blocked Ada's tunnel to Her Nextdoor's onion patch. Still, added Ada, she's a bit dramatic don't you think, bit highly strung! She needs a crispy dry one, added Horny Frank.
    5.3 Spencer: Spencer asked what else happened with the black cat? Nothing much, replied Ada, the black cat just sits on his special branch and waits for the long tails to appear from their tunnels, and he pounces and gives them what for. Which ones, the RLT or the UDFF? asked Beardy. That's the beauty of it, replied Ada, the black cat doesn't care, he says if it looks like a long tail, smells like a long tail, has a long tail, then it's a long tail and it gets what for. We really need to organise a meet-up

with Ben the Long Tail or Foxy the foxy nosed Fox and see what's going on insisted Spencer.

5.4 Beardy: Beardy stated that's probably why the railway verge area has been so quiet lately. Karen the Sheep has gone, there's no long tail types around, no foxy nosed fox types around. The Big Foreign Bird has disappeared again; even the peckers stay put. Maybe Ada and Spud should stay put too, it's all getting a bit weird out there. No way stated Ada, we can't be dictated to by the People from up Town. The black cat only seemed interested in the long tails, he never bothered Ada at all, in fact, he was quite friendly to be honest, added Ada. Beardy stated that he will try and put the word out tonight to tell the foxy nosed fox types that we want a meet-up as soon as.

5.5 Horny Frank: Horny Frank stated that it's good having the long tails kept in their place, so no probs with him. You say that Horny Frank, argued Spencer, but for some reason, the People from up Town and Those from The Farm want the railway verge area cleared, and we don't know why. The black cat is obviously a professional and is contracted to keep the long tails out of the railway verge area, so that's all he's interested in because that's the contract. He wasn't interested in Ada because she's not in the contract. Not sure argued, Horny Frank, the black cat couldn't give Ada what for even if he wanted to! Too right, agreed Ada, no chance, he never moved from his wee safe special branch. Don't be so sure, stated Spud, these black cats from up Town are specially trained to dish out some serious what for to anything. Ada added that the black cat had Spud clocked the other day too, he watched us when we were on our impromptu mission to The Farm. He said you were a big boy, and that you could probably handle yourself. Too right, said Spud, he is a big boy, and he can handle himself, and the black cat's wee safe special branch won't save him either.

6. Other business – None

40. REGAN FROM THE SPECIAL BRANCH

40th Lockdown Board Meeting: Wed, 29th April 2020

In Attendance:

Me (Chair)

Spud II (Head of cat dept)

Spencer (Head of bigger dog dept)

Ada (Head of smaller dog dept)

Horny Frank (Head of horny rabbit dept)

Beardy (Head of not so horny rabbit dept)

Apologies - None

Call to order 06:00hrs

1. There were sufficient members for a quorum
2. Minutes of previous meeting approved
3. Business from last meeting: None
4. Statement from the Chair: Boris's mate Matt stated that all Care Home staff can now get tested for the virus, so that's good. Dr Alan from UCLH states that Cannabis helps with pain during these

stressful times, so that's good too. The Times stated that Care Homes are in a worse situation than hospitals, so that's not good.

5. Business Updates:
   5.1 Beardy: Beardy stated that he had a chat with one of the foxy nosed Fox types who turned up in the garden area last night. Beardy told the foxy nosed fox types that the Board would like to arrange a meet-up with Ben the Long Tail and Foxy the foxy nosed Fox. They said they would pass the message on and get back to him tonight. They also stated that there's a few of the Special Branch black cats managing the railway verge area now, they don't tend to bother them as much the foxy nosed fox type explained, the leader is called Regan, nasty piece of work, they're up to no good that's for sure. Plus, Beardy added, apparently Roger the Long Tail is an up Town employee too, but he's only a foot soldier though, there's probably a Boss as well.
   5.2 Spud: Spud stated, so there's more than one then, that's interesting, and the long tails have a group in up Town as well, with a Boss! Nevertheless, this Regan from the Special Branch needs to be dealt with. We can't have him roaming up and down the railway verge area acting like he runs the show. Therefore, Spud added, he's going to go on his own special black ops and hunt down Regan from the Special Branch and give him what for. Attack is the best form of defence, Spud added.
   5.3 Ada: Ada stated that she'd go with Spud for back up just in case there's loads of them. Ok, said Spud, but keep your distance, this is his fight. Ada stated that he wondered what Princess Snickerdoodle's take on all this was. Beardy stated that he thinks she would be extremely worried, with the RLT, the UDFF, and now another dodgy group from up Town, with a Boss. Where is the Principality of Snickerdoodle anyway, is it an actual area? asked Beardy. That's my point, replied Ada, is it under the railway verge way area, is it under decking in garden areas, is it all just one big underground network? We know very little about her added Ada.
   5.4 Spencer: Spencer stated that Spud should be careful and definitely take Ada with him. You don't know what their end game is so it's hard to judge what they're capable off. We need to have a proper butchers at that Snickerdoodle agreement again, Spencer continued, it was fishy then and still fishy now, but for the moment we need to be seen to be going along with

it until we get an understanding of what the actual end game is and who's involved.

5.5 Horny Frank: Horny Frank stated that they're bad luck as well. Who's bad luck? asked Ada. The black cats, Horny Frank replied, they steal your soul and every witch has one. How many witches do you know? asked Ada. None, but that's not the point, argued Horny Frank. What is your point? asked Spud. Well said Horny Frank, my point is that they're evil and they cast nasty spells. This should be brilliant, go on then, Ada insisted. It's so true, Horny Frank argued, and there's a story to prove it. Is there now? replied Ada. Yes, there is, Horny Frank continued. Many many years ago, on a moonless night, a daddy rabbit and his kid were hopping home from doing a bit of hunting when a black cat type came across their path. They give it a good what for, and it ran off into a nearby house of a woman who was at the time, being accused of being a witch. Hang on a minute, interrupted Spud, a rabbit giving a black cat what for, are you sure you're not having a wee wobbly moment? No, it's the absolute truth, remember that the rabbit's kid was there too, a big buck he was, well trained in giving black cat types what for, Horny Frank insisted. Anyway, the very next day, the daddy rabbit and his big buck of a kid saw the woman who lived in the house, and she was limping and bruised. So what? said Spud. Well you see, replied Horny Frank, the black cat was, in fact, the woman, and she was bruised because she had been given what for the night before by the daddy rabbit and his big buck of a kid. So, said Spud, the black cat turned into a woman? No, argued Horny Frank, the woman turned into the black cat! What a complete load of betty swollocks replied Ada.

6. Other business – None

41. HER NEXTDOOR AND LULU

41st Lockdown Board Meeting: Thurs, 30th April 2020

In Attendance:

Me (Chair)

Spud II (Head of cat dept)

Spencer (Head of bigger dog dept)

Ada (Head of smaller dog dept)

Horny Frank (Head of horny rabbit dept)

Beardy (Head of not so horny rabbit dept)

Apologies - None

Call to order 06:00hrs

1. There were sufficient members for a quorum
2. Minutes of previous meeting approved
3. Business from last meeting: None
4. Statement from the Chair: Boris's bouncing baby boy arrived yesterday, so that's good. Boris is calling his bouncing baby boy Dave after Winston Churchill, maybe, so that's funny. Boris's mate

Matt stated that the - 100,000 per day test target, will be achieved by COP today, so that's funny too.

5. Business Updates:

   5.1 Spud: Spud stated that straight after the meeting yesterday, he got ready and went over the perimeter area between the garden area and the railway verge area and headed East up along the railway verge area toward up Town. The morning started pretty cold, and the undergrowth and thick thickets were wet and horrible, but by the time he arrived at the busted sofa the sun was out again, and he could feel the heat on his face, which was nice. The area was all free from activity, even the tree, where the Special Branch hang out was empty. He stayed focused for a bit then decided to have a sneaky snooze on the busted sofa. However, the snooze was short lived as he was awakened by a long tail who introduced himself as Roger.

   5.2 Beardy: Beardy asked was it the Roger the Long Tail who visited him the other night, the one with the missing passport? Apparently it was, replied Spud. Did he ask after his passport? asked Beardy. No, he never mentioned it, replied Spud. He just wanted a quick chat, continued Spud. What did he want then? insisted Beardy. Well he wanted stuff, replied Spud. What kind of stuff? asked Beardy. Not sure really, when Regan of the Special Branch knocks off for lunch, Roger the Long Tail holds the fort. However, he doesn't mind if the RLT have a wee run around as long as they give him stuff. Roger the Long Tail added, that because Spud was there by their tunnel entrances, the RLT won't show themselves, so he can't collect any stuff, which therefore means Spud owes Roger the Long Tail, stuff! What kind of stuff? Beardy repeated. No idea, Spud stated again, he gave Roger the Long Tail a serious what for and sent him off with his skinny long tail between his legs and told him to go bash the bishop.

   5.3 Ada: Ada stated that that sorted that then. Are you going back for Regan of the Special Branch again? He Definitely was replied Spud. So, this Roger the Long Tail is in the 'garbage business' then? Looks that way, agreed Spud. Excellent stuff, that's all we need replied Ada, Roger all mobbed up. Mobbed-up Roger is probably on some sort of initiation on his way to becoming a made long tail. Well this is going to piss him off if he can't pay tribute to his Boss, said Beardy. It looks like we're heading somewhere very interesting now, stated Ada.

   5.4 Spencer: Spencer stated that that's all we need, mobbed-up long tails, you couldn't write this stuff! We haven't heard the last of Mobbed-up Roger, so we need to be extra vigilant now. We have no idea how Mobbed-up Roger and his cronies are linked to any of this, other than his racketeering in the railway verge area. For example, why was his passport found near the incredible machine? Spencer added. Any word from Ben the Long Tail or Foxy the foxy nosed Fox yet? asked Spencer. Nothing yet, replied Beardy, in fact last night was very quiet all round. Spencer stated that he didn't like all this quietness, there's lots going on at this party, and we haven't been invited!

5.5 Horny Frank: Horny Frank asked if Spencer was referring to the party in the garden area yesterday at the crispy table? What party? replied Spencer. Her Nextdoor turned up with Lulu, for a crispy dry one. No way stated Ada. Way, replied Horny Frank, sat right there right at the crispy dry table as cocky as you like. No sooner had the sun come out, Her Nextdoor turned up, all smiles, butter wouldn't melt, friendly as you like, and was given a crispy dry one. Where was the Nextdoor Kid then? asked Ada. Maybe it turned into Lulu, Beardy laughed. Ada stated that it's more likely that the Nextdoor Kid had probably gone out with Him Nextdoor maybe, and while he's away Her Nextdoor gets her Lulu out. How did he miss all this? asked Spencer. Well, Spud was on special black ops while Spencer and Ada were on patrol in the perimeter area and the railway verge area replied Horny Frank. It was a quickie, all over in about an hour and a half. Who and what is Lulu? asked Spud. One of your crowd, replied Horny Frank, tasty too, probably!

6. Other business – None

42. THE CAMP FOLLOWER POLICY

42nd Lockdown Board Meeting: Fri, 1st May 2020

In Attendance:

Me (Chair)

Spud II (Head of cat dept)

Spencer (Head of bigger dog dept)

Ada (Head of smaller dog dept)

Horny Frank (Head of horny rabbit dept)

Beardy (Head of not so horny rabbit dept)

Apologies - None

Call to order 06:00hrs

1. There were sufficient members for a quorum
2. Minutes of previous meeting approved
3. Business from last meeting: None

4. Statement from the Chair: Boris stated yesterday that we are – past the peak, so that's good. Boris also stated that - we can now see the sunlight, but we need to keep the R number below 1, so that's good too. Paulin Kola from the BBC stated that the BBC reporters have worked very hard and deserve the clap, so that's catchy.
5. Business Updates:
    5.1 Spud: Spud stated that he couldn't believe we let another cat into the garden area, and she got to sit at the Chair's crispy table, unbelievable! Spud stated that he's not even allowed anywhere near the crispy table in the afternoon! Her Nextdoor turns up, showing off her Lulu and gets a crispy dry one. To be fair, replied the Chair, Her Nextdoor turned up and said she felt a bit guilty about giving him an ear-bashing the other day over Ada and the toy incident. As a token of goodwill, she brought with her a bottle of crispy dry, and it just so happened she produced her Lulu as well, it would be rude not to, the Chair added. By the way, the Chair continued, Her Nextdoor is only minding Lulu for a Girl up Town.
    5.2 Ada: Ada stated that while Spud was going on about Her Nextdoor's Lulu, Ada thought she'd explained what happened yesterday regarding another special operation in the railway verge area. Shortly after the meeting yesterday, Spud and Ada headed out on another mission in the railway verge area. They intended to go East toward up Town again, but this time stay closer together. They were sure the busted sofa area wouldn't be so quiet this time. They never got very far when they had a brush-pass with none other than Foxy the foxy nosed Fox and Ben the Long Tail. They both said that Spud and Ada shouldn't go anywhere near the busted sofa area, it's crawling with the Special Branch, and Mobbed-up Roger is there too with a cell from the RLT.
    5.3 Spencer: Spencer stated that it was interesting that Mobbed-up Roger was running with the RLT, looks like he's going for an upgrade and run a wee family of his own, he's walking on very thin ice if that's his plan, but that could work to our advantage. What else did they say? asked Spencer. Couple of things, replied Ada, first was the Snickerdoodle agreement, Princess Snickerdoodle wants it signed before any more collaboration. Secondly, Foxy the foxy nosed Fox stated, that from the Intel they gathered from The Farm via Karen the Sheep, People from up Town are planning on partitioning the railway verge area, at the middle point between up Town and Elsewhere, which happens to be smack bang right outside the

Board's garden area. So, asked Ada, they plan to create a border in the railway verge area right at our garden area? That's correct said Foxy the foxy nosed Fox; Ben the Long Tail nodded in agreement.

5.4 Horny Frank: Horny Frank asked on a slightly different note, would it be possible for Ada to refrain from entering the rabbit-run and the hutch when the run-gate is left open. That's his and Horny Frank's quality time indoors; only it's outdoors at the moment. It's not an Ada quality time for her to run about their run area wreaking havoc. Ada stated that she thought that Horny Frank was having a ball. Horny Frank argued that he was absolutely not having a ball, Ada just chased him all over the run, in and out of the hutch, it was a very unpleasant experience. Ada insisted that it was great fun and she was only trying to tag him as she was *It*.

5.5 Beardy: Beardy stated that if Lulu belonged to a Girl from up Town, do we know anything about her or what she wants from her time? We don't even know much about Her Nextdoor, never mind the girl from up Town. So for all we know, Lulu could be an asset from up Town, handled by the girl from up Town, who places Lulu with Her Nextdoor, Her Nextdoor has the easy job of entertaining the Chair with a crispy dry one, next thing you know there's a bit of crispy dry table-top talk, the Chair spills the load and Lulu captures it all. Honey Trap 101. Well stated the Chair, that's an interesting load of furry plumbs, but no need to panic Mr Mainwaring, because Her Indoors knows now, she found a long blond hair on my cotoneaster and all hell broke loose. The Chair said that she asked if it belonged to the camp follower from next door. Anyway, added the Chair, it wasn't a pretty sight, and now we have a new 'No Camp Follower Policy' we need to get signed off today.

6. Other business – None

43. ULTRASONIC FREQUENCIES

43rd Lockdown Board Meeting: Sat, 2nd May 2020

In Attendance:

Me (Chair)

Spud II (Head of cat dept)

Spencer (Head of bigger dog dept)

Ada (Head of smaller dog dept)

Horny Frank (Head of horny rabbit dept)

Beardy (Head of not so horny rabbit dept)

Apologies - None

Call to order 06:00hrs

1. There were sufficient members for a quorum
2. Minutes of previous meeting approved

3. Business from last meeting: The 'no camp followers policy' was agreed and will be active with immediate effect.
4. End of the Week Statement from the Chair: We have been in lockdown now for six weeks! I want to thank all departments for their cooperation during these stressful times. Our lovable Stakeholders are all complete lunatics now, but still happy to continue to read the ramblings of another lunatic. So, we will go on for a bit longer. The Lockdown continues but seems to be easing somewhat, apparently, we're past the peak and there's light at the end of the tunnel, so chin up, not long to go now.
5. Statement from the Chair: Boris's mate Matt stated that he hit his '100,000 tests per day' target, so that's interesting. Mr Ashworth stated that Boris's mate Matt is a wee cheat, so that's not good. Boris is planning a 'road map' for exiting lockdown, so that's good.
6. Business Updates:
    6.1 Spencer: Spencer stated that he had a butchers at Princess Snickerdoodle's agreement yesterday. Anything good? asked Ada. Well, there are some interesting points we should discuss today and make a decision if possible. There's a series of sensible compromises that can enable all sides to claim some wins over the others, without actually winning anything, but everybody saves face. The long tails ultrasound frequencies will be given official status, plus facilities will be provided for these noises to be communicated at any future meetings.
    6.2 Spud: Spud stated that if everybody wins and saves face, then that's cool, but never knew the long tails used ultrasonic frequencies. Well, why would you, replied Ada, when was the last time you were at a meeting with a long tail and decided to communicate using ultrasonic frequencies. Anyway, Spencer continued, to help ease humiliation, the foxy nosed foxes have a veto over some of the changes the long tails insist on Ultrasound frequency, for example, won't be taught to any foxy nosed fox kids, nor will it be used for signposts. How can you use ultrasonic frequencies for signposts? asked Ada. No idea, replied Spencer, he didn't write it, he's just reading it. Is that it then? asked Ada. Well that seems to be the gist of it, replied Spencer. Well count her out, replied Ada, she's not signing that, it's nothing but a load of flimflammery.
    6.3 Beardy: Beardy asked, how does the Board benefit from it? Well, Spencer replied, there'll be peace in the railway verge area between us, the foxy nosed foxes, and the long tails. Yes, but so what, argued Ada, the railway verge area is going to partitioned with a border right outside our garden area,

movement will be restricted anyway, how's the agreement going to address that? Beardy agreed with Ada and stated that he was out too.

6.4 Horny Frank: Horny Frank asked if there's a border right outside our garden area; when Spud or Ada go over the perimeter area between the garden area and the railway verge area, which side of the border are they on? That's my point exactly, stated Ada, we're caught between a rock and a hard place, but hey ho, we all win, and our faces are saved, and the long tails can make funny noises at meetings! Horny Frank stated that he doesn't understand any of it, so he's out too.

6.5 Ada: Ada stated that on another note, which is a million times more interesting, she went on another secret black ops mission in the railway verge area yesterday. And again, stated Spencer, a mission without Board agreement! It was a secret mission argued Ada, can't be a secret if everybody knows about it. Anyway, Ada continued, she now understands why the railway verge area is so-called. Why's that then? asked Horny Frank. Well, she spotted a railway line. She went over the perimeter area between the garden area, and the railway verge area and instead of going East or West as usual, she went North, and low and behold she came to a dead end. What did you see? Ada said that she saw a fence, and beyond the fence was a railway line, complete with a train. You must have known there was a railway line close by, stated Spencer, you were collecting the food thrown from the train to feed your prisoners. She knew that replied Ada, just never pieced it all together. So, Ada continued, that's not the big news. She went along the railway fence way, East toward up Town, which was easier, as the thick thickets weren't so thick along the railway fence way, then went back into the thickety thickets heading South, toward the busted sofa area. The busted sofa area was all clear again, which was interesting in itself, but that's still not the big news said Ada. So what's the big news then? insisted Horny Frank. Just between the railway fence way and the busted sofa area, she found a mountain of treasure! What kind of treasure? It was amazing, loads and loads of wonderful things, said Ada. That's brilliant, said Horny Frank, can you bring it back? Well there's so much of it she'll need help, said Ada. We can help, replied Spud, let's set up a mission to go and retrieve the treasure later today if the coast is clear of course.

7. Other business – None

44. THE TREASURE

44th Lockdown Board Meeting: Sun, 3rd May 2020

In Attendance:

Me (Chair)

Spud II (Head of cat dept)

Spencer (Head of bigger dog dept)

Ada (Head of smaller dog dept)

Horny Frank (Head of horny rabbit dept)

Beardy (Head of not so horny rabbit dept)

Apologies - None

Call to order 06:00hrs

1. There were sufficient members for a quorum
2. Minutes of previous meeting approved
3. Business from last meeting: The Princess Snickerdoodle Agreement was rejected by the Board.

4. Statement from the Chair: Deputy CMO Dr Jenny stated that hospital admissions due to the virus is down by 13%, so that's good. The new Nightingale hospitals weren't needed after all, so that's good. Covid Toe is now a thing, so that's not so good.
5. Business Updates:
    5.1 Spud: Spud stated that the mission to the Treasure was a complete waste of time yesterday, nothing but a load of old rubbish. Sounds like it was just fly-tipping, stated Spencer. Definitely was, replied Spud. Hang on a minute, argued Ada, there was loads of great stuff to play with, it was even great just playing on the mound of goodies itself! It's just rubbish, reiterated Spud, you're starting to sound like a slumdog recycler. What's wrong with recycling? asked Ada. Everything, stated Spud, it's filthy for one, you're starting to smell like the long tail rag-picker.
    5.2 Spencer: Spencer stated that we should report it to be fair. Report it to who? asked Beardy. Well, replied Spencer, there's a council department called FixMyRailwayVergeArea, we could report it to them. How do they fly-tip in railway verge area anyway, asked Beardy, the Northern end is blocked by the railway line complete with trains, and the Southern end is blocked with garden areas? Well, as the rubbish seems to appear the closer you get to up Town, maybe it comes in from there, suggested Spud. Maybe said Spencer, but there's the incredible machine near the peckers garden area on the way to Elsewhere too, and that's a pretty large piece of machinery, how did that get there? So, the incredible machine is rubbish too? argued Ada. Well it kinda is, said Spencer. Don't believe you lot, replied Ada, everything has value! Ok Jamal, don't get your gunties in a twist, replied Spud.
    5.3 Beardy: Beardy stated that he had a brush-pass with the foxy nosed foxes last night in the garden area. He gave them back the unsigned Princess Snickerdoodle Agreement and told them the Board isn't interested in ultrasonic frequencies, nor saving face. The foxy nosed foxes didn't look very happy, added Beardy. Who cares, replied Spud, they're all up to no good anyway, he doesn't believe for one moment that the long tails, nor the foxy nosed Foxes are interested in our wellbeing, so they can go and kiss my kitchen door cat flap.
    5.4 Horny Frank: Horny Frank stated that he noticed Her Indoors spent a lot of time in the garden area yesterday. Well, it's always nice to see Her Indoors outdoors, said Spencer, and it was such a lovely day, the sun was shining, the crispy dry was

flowing. Her Indoors isn't fond of the crispy dry though, argued Horny Frank. That makes sense, said Ada. However, the crispy dry was still flowing, repeated Spencer, albeit in one direction. Well, it's good to see Her Indoors anyway, replied Horny Frank, we don't see enough of her. Ada stated that Spencer and she get to see Her Indoors every night for their quality cuddle hour when she snuggles up watching her wee soaps. That's lovely, said Horny Frank, he and Beardy only get to see Her Indoors once a month, when she's cleaning up the scoot from their comfort zone. Spud stated that, as a rule, he ignores her most of the time.

5.5 Ada: Ada stated that Her Indoors spending more time in the garden area is a bad thing. Like us, she obviously doesn't trust Her Nextdoor, added Ada. She was parading up and down that fence area between our garden area, and Her Nextdoor's garden area and it wasn't because she was eyeballing Her Nextdoor's cabbage patch. No, Ada continued, Her Indoors wants to give Her Nextdoor a good seeing to. Don't you mean what for? corrected Beardy. Whatever replied Ada. Horny Frank chipped in that both sounded good. The point is, we need to keep Her Nextdoor on good terms, for the sake of potential Intel, stated Ada. Yes, but there's the 'no camp follower' policy in play now, which scuppers everything, replied Beardy. That was Her Indoors' policy too, and she's not even a member of the Board, she makes too many policies for a non-board member, stated Ada, we need a create a policy about her policymaking. She should only be allowed to create policies regarding indoor stuff, like the kitchen door and flap policy for example, which was fair enough, but her garden area involvement should be curtailed- just saying, said Ada. Good luck with that interrupted the Chair. Does Her Indoors have a problem with the girl from up Town too? asked Ada. Are you mad, replied the Chair, Her Indoors knows nothing about the girl from up Town! Well that's good, replied Ada, because the 'no camp follower' policy therefore, doesn't apply to the girl from up Town, and by default, her Lulu, and we need information from her, via her Lulu, because we currently know nothing about anything and that needs to change sharpish! So, insisted Ada, the Chair needs to get word to Her Nextdoor to tell her that he would like some dialogical intercourse with the girl from up Town's Lulu, and could she arrange a meet-up.

6. Other business – None

45. DOWNTOWN BOY

45th Lockdown Board Meeting: Mon, 4th May 2020

In Attendance:

Me (Chair)

Spud II (Head of cat dept)

Spencer (Head of bigger dog dept)

Ada (Head of smaller dog dept)

Horny Frank (Head of horny rabbit dept)

Beardy (Head of not so horny rabbit dept)

Apologies - None

Call to order 06:00hrs

1. There were sufficient members for a quorum
2. Minutes of previous meeting approved
3. Business from last meeting: None

4. Statement from the Chair: Boris will introduce a - whack-a-mole plan, so that's funny. Boris will also inform us this week when Lockdown easing will start, so that's good. Italy reopens today, so that's interesting.
5. Business Updates:
    5.1 Spencer: Spencer stated that he'd like to thank the Chair for having the brush-pass with Her Nextdoor, and for arranging the meet-up with the Girl from up Town's Lulu yesterday. Spencer added that he appreciates that this was not easy for the Chair, considering the current circumstances relating to Her Indoors 'no camp follower' policy. The Chair stated that the 'no camp follower' policy was not breached, as Her Nextdoor never came into the Board's garden area. Clever stuff, interrupted Horny Frank, so Her Indoors has no grievance then? The Chair stated that he wouldn't go as far as saying that, as Her Indoors doesn't actually know about the brush-pass, as it was merely just an over the fence conflab, so it wasn't even a thing.
    5.2 Beardy: Beardy asked, was there a crispy dry one involved in this 'not even a thing' thing by the garden fence? No definitely not, insisted the Chair, well not with Her Nextdoor anyway, he just said good morning to her as she attended her cabbage patch. Always like to watch the way she handles her brassicas, it's art personified, added the Chair. Fair enough, said Beardy, but what did she say about the Girl from up Town's Lulu? Well, continued the Chair, after Her Nextdoor let me sample her pak choy, which he must say was divine, the Chair mentioned that Spud was sorry he missed the Girl from up Town's Lulu the other day and would like a visit.
    5.3 Spud: Spud stated that he was slightly put out about the 'Spud would like a visit' comment. He didn't want the Girl from up Town's Lulu to think that coition was on the cards, because of course, it isn't, because he doesn't have any beanbags, they were removed when he was a youngster, without his consent he might add! As it happens, she lost her egg maker as a youngster too, so although coition was definitely off the cards, we did have that in common, not your usual chat-up line, but it worked.
    5.4 Horny Frank: Horny Frank interrupted and stated, ok Romeo, what did she say about anything other than missing bits and pieces? It's not funny argued Spud, he's the only Board member that's been chopped, which in itself amounts to discrimination, but let's just park that issue for a rainy day.

However, Spud continued, the Girl from up Town's Lulu said that she does have some Intel that might interest the Board. Apparently, the Girl from up Town doesn't really get involved in politics, but her husband is high up in the Corporation in up Town. Spud added that the Girl from up Town is from money, but her husband, on the other hand, is only a downtown boy made good.

- 5.5 Ada: Ada stated that that was excellent news, so Downtown Boy is in the career business and has a high place in the Corporation now, that has to be good. What's the Corporation? asked Ada. Well, the Corporation is run by the People from up Town, but this is the interesting bit, the Corporation also controls The Farm. That is interesting, replied Ada, why would the Corporation want The Farm? No idea replied Spud. Spencer stated that whatever the reason, the railway verge area is caught up in the middle somehow. At least we're on to something good now, stated Ada, we have an agent in up Town that's connected to the People from the Corporation via the Girl from up Town's Downtown boy. So Spud, it's your job to keep the Girl from up Town's Lulu sweet as Ada continued. Definitely, insisted Spencer, it's our only way to get a handle on what's going on in the railway verge area and understand all the players better. We can't let the long tails nor the foxy nosed foxes know any of this, stated Beardy. Hundred per cent agreed Spencer. Well the Girl from up Town's Lulu is pleasant enough, said Spud, and he will try his best. It's a reverse Honey Trap stated Ada- you can do it. Yes, replied Spud, but it's a Honey Trap without the Honey, isn't it? Fake it, said Ada, go through the motions. Spud argued that he doesn't even know what the motions are! Horny Frank told Spud not to worry, he would give him some valuable lessons. If he comes near me with that leaky hose, he'll rip him a new one, insisted Spud!
6. Other business – None

46. THE COUNCIL OF FIVE

46th Lockdown Board Meeting: Tues, 5th May 2020

In Attendance:

Me (Chair)

Spud II (Head of cat dept)

Spencer (Head of bigger dog dept)

Ada (Head of smaller dog dept)

Horny Frank (Head of horny rabbit dept)

Beardy (Head of not so horny rabbit dept)

Apologies - None

Lockdown Board Meetings 2020

Call to order 06:00hrs

1. There were sufficient members for a quorum
2. Minutes of previous meeting approved
3. Business from last meeting: None
4. Statement from the Chair: Scientists state that the 47D11 antibody targets the SARS-CoV-2's protein as well, and therefore stops it from functioning, so that's good. Boris's mate Matt stated yesterday that the Isle of Wight is the - test, track and trace programme's guinea pigs, so that's good too. New Zealand's Jacinda stated that they had beaten the virus, but - it has a long tail, so that's different.
5. Business Updates:
    5.1 Spud: Spud stated that he was slightly concerned about what Lulu was saying yesterday with regards to the up Town Corporation, and this planned border malarkey. This got him thinking, added Spud if the up Town Corporation sets up a border between up Town and Elsewhere, it suggests that they both claim control over both sections of the railway verge area. Spud added that Karen the Sheep did try to warn us about this if he remembers correctly. She did replied Beardy she said that they were sticking up poles in the railway verge area near up Town, because if you remember, we thought they were robbing Polish types, but they were only these big metal poles in the ground, and Karen the Sheep was saying that they are there to fry our brains and lungs.
    5.2 Beardy: Beardy stated that on top of all that, he had another brush-pass with the foxy nosed fox types last night again. They really are worried about not having the Princess Snickerdoodle Agreement signed off and want to know what our red-lines were, and maybe negotiate further to resolve the impasse. However, we chatted for a bit afterwards, continued Beardy, and they said that the up Town Corporation has officially declared the existence of the Border now, and call it the 209 Meridian, and it's in the railway verge area exactly between the Board's garden area and Her Nextdoor's garden area. So, Beardy added, that means if we enter the railway verge area, we are East of the 209 Meridian, and if Her Nextdoor enters the railway area, she is West of the 209 Meridian.
    5.3 Horny Frank: Horny Frank stated that it's doing his brain in just thinking about it! What happens now if we go into the railway verge area on the East side and cross over into the

West side? Well nothing at the moment, supposes Beardy, it's not a physical border yet, but he guesses that could well change soon, and probably manned by that Regan of the Special Branch no doubt. The foxy nosed fox types also stated, Beardy continued, that the up Town Corporation is starting to tidy up the railway verge area near up Town, calling it the Beautification Project, which no doubt will continue right down to the 209 Meridian. Well that's a good thing surely, said Horny Frank, it's a right mess at the moment.

5.4 Ada: Ada stated that the Beautification of the railway verge area is definitely not a good thing. It's home to thousands of little wee creature types who will end up as refugees, and head over the Border at the 209 Meridian to some smelly camp run by Oxfam International. Not to mention all the recent treasure she found, added Ada, Oxfam won't replace that! The big question is, continued Ada, what does Elsewhere think of all this new activity? We know very little about up Town and this Corporation, but we know even less about Elsewhere. Ada added that she thinks the Board should agree on a special op today, to go over the 209 Meridian before it becomes physical, and head as far as they can West toward Elsewhere, and see what's there. She suggested that she and Spencer go.

5.5 Spencer: Spencer stated that he agrees with the special op, and they should head off early, before the food-run and after morning ablutions. On another note, Spencer continued, with regards to the Princess Snickerdoodle Agreement, the Board should introduce their red line. Spencer suggests that before they agree to anything with anybody, they need reassurances of trust first. In light of the current situation with this stressful human flu, the newly formed 209 Meridian Border, and now the Beautification Project, Spencer wants to set up a War Council of Five members. The Board will nominate Spud as our ambassador, because according to the Chair, Spud won the latest Stakeholder Poll, he is currently the Stakeholders' favourite. We will invite Ben the Long Tail, Foxy the foxy nosed Fox who can represent East of the 209, and invite Gregory the Pecker who can represent West of the 209. That's only four, argued Horny Frank, you said it's a Council of Five. This is our chance to get ahead of the game, replied Spencer, we will invite Lulu as the fifth member, we will say that she's Her Nextdoor's Lulu and not the Girl from up Town's Lulu, and as the railway verge area outside Her Nextdoor's garden area is now West of the 209 Meridian border, Lulu can represent the West along with Gregory the Pecker, however, in actual fact, she is our very own special agent, so we have leverage in the newly formed Council of Five. Excellent agreed Spud. Horny Frank asked where he came in the poll? 3rd out of 21, replied the Chair, just behind Ada and in front of Spencer. Back of the net replied Horny Frank, what a result.

6. Other business – None

47. PARADISE

47th Lockdown Board Meeting: Wed, 6th May 2020

In Attendance:

Me (Chair)

Spud II (Head of cat dept)

Spencer (Head of bigger dog dept)

Ada (Head of smaller dog dept)

Horny Frank (Head of horny rabbit dept)

Beardy (Head of not so horny rabbit dept)

Apologies - None

Lockdown Board Meetings 2020

Call to order 06:00hrs

1. There were sufficient members for a quorum
2. Minutes of previous meeting approved
3. Business from last meeting: None
4. Statement from the Chair: Boris's mate Mr Ferguson, the lockdown king, introduces a new Government position that isn't advisory, so that's good. Boris's other mate Mr Raab stated yesterday that the UK is now leading the way at the top of the European virus table, so that's not good. Cambridge University's, Prof. Spiegelhalter, stated that Mr Raab's numbers are substantially underestimated, so that can't be good.
5. Business Updates:
    5.1 Spencer: Spencer stated that shortly after morning ablutions yesterday, he headed over the perimeter area between the garden area and the railway verge area and headed West towards Elsewhere. He crossed over the virtual Border at the 209 Meridian, it was currently all quiet, apart from the distant sound coming from the West that reminded him of one of Ada's soft toys being squeezed to death. Beardy asked why Ada didn't go with him? Spencer replied that after the meeting yesterday, Ada was a bit poorly. Ada argued that she only had a touch of the collywobbles and was squirting a bit, but Spencer thought it best if she stayed behind. Bit nervous were you? asked Horny Frank. You can go foxtrot yourself, replied Ada.
    5.2 Ada: Ada stated that she must've eaten something bad yesterday morning! Every time he sees her, replied Spencer, she's always got something in her mouth, even hard guff, like what's that all about! Things just need collecting, argued Ada, they're just left lying around, and it annoys her compulsive brain. What's a compulsive brain? asked Horny Frank. It's a wee voice in my head that says, 'pick it up, pick it up,' drives me nuts, Ada replied. Even hard guff? asked Beardy. Yes, insisted Ada, the Chair isn't great at clearing it up during these stressful times, makes the place look somewhat uncouth, then her wee voice starts, 'pick it up, pick it up!'
    5.3 Horny Frank: Horny Frank stated that that's mad, is that why she was in their rabbit-run the other day was she going to rearrange their doo-doo? What is it with you lot, Ada interrupted, she had an upset tummy yesterday, and hard guff may or may not have attributed to that, but take a chill pill for

God's sake, she went into the rabbit-run to play It, not to feng shui it.

5.4 Spud: Spud stated that he had sent word, via the foxy nosed fox types, about the formation of the Council of Five, before the Board contemplates signing the Princess Snickerdoodle Agreement. He was just waiting for word back. Spud also stated that they need the message to get to Lulu as well, which the Chair can pass on, no doubt, during a crispy dry one later, maybe. They also need to communicate with Gregory the Pecker Spud added. Job done, replied Spencer. On his mission to Elsewhere he stopped outside the peckers' garden area and Gregory the Pecker came out to greet him. The peckers don't frequent the railway verge area much anymore after the pecker kids' incident. He did, however, introduce Spencer to another pecker who was the new head pecker of all the peckers, and after a brief spat of clucking, the new head pecker thanked the Board for saving the pecker kids, so that was all very nice. Spencer stated that he told the peckers about the Council of Five, and it was agreed that Gregory the Pecker would be a member. Spencer also found out from the peckers, that the weird squeaky toy sound he had heard earlier, was a horned coot that sometimes attacks the pecker kids and missus Pecker's wee eggs. Those pecker kids get it rough, added Ada, hopefully, the new Peckerhead will sort these issues out going forward. Hopefully, replied Spencer, but on a brighter note though, after leaving Peckerhead, he continued West toward Elsewhere. He walked for another couple of klicks until all of a sudden, the thickety thickets thinned, and he found himself in paradise. It was beautiful, explained Spencer. No more rubbish nor busted sofas, no beautification required at all, it was already beautiful, a masterpiece of form and colour just as nature intended. Sounds breath-taking, replied Beardy, what did you do? Nothing, replied Spencer, just rested for a bit, soaking up the enchantment of nature, then had a wee wander through the feathered grasses, listening to a cacophony of cricket types. But it was getting late; he lost time talking to the clucking Peckerhead, so he had to head back. But we must go there again soon insisted Spencer.

5.5 Beardy: Beardy stated that he noticed Venus was very bright in the sky this morning. Was it? replied Ada.

6. Other business – None

48. LOKO FOKO

48th Lockdown Board Meeting: Thurs, 7th May 2020

In Attendance:

Me (Chair)

Spud II (Head of cat dept)

Spencer (Head of bigger dog dept)

Ada (Head of smaller dog dept)

Horny Frank (Head of horny rabbit dept)

Beardy (Head of not so horny rabbit dept)

Apologies - None

Call to order 06:00hrs

1. There were sufficient members for a quorum
2. Minutes of previous meeting approved
3. Business from last meeting: None

4. Statement from the Chair: Boris will let us know today about the easing of the lockdown restrictions, so that's good. The BBC's Nick Triggle asked, is it time to free the healthy? so that's waspish. Boris stated yesterday that the NHS is doing a great job, but Care Home staff need training on the proper use of PPE, so that's even more waspish.
5. Business Updates:
    5.1 Spud: Spud stated that all the suggested members of the Council of Five have been contacted and have agreed to participate and meet on a regular basis. The first Council meeting is to take place later today. Unfortunately, it will have to take place during crispy dry time, but hopefully will not interfere with the Chair's 'me time' too much. The Chair stated that that's ok and that he understands how hard it is to get all the members together and hopes the music and his singing won't bother them too much. The Chair also stated that a lot of our wonderful Stakeholders, who are utterly loko foko now, are concerned about the safety of Karen the Sheep, and could Spud put the loko foko's concern on today's agenda?
    5.2 Beardy: Beardy stated that it was great news the Council of Five is up and running today, and in such a short space of time too. He also stated that he agreed about highlighting the issue regarding Karen the Sheep, and something should definitely be done to help her. Spud agreed and stated that there isn't an agenda for today's first meeting, as it's mainly about setting out our objectives, but will definitely table Karen the Sheep's plight, and hopefully get an action. Spud also stated that he was in the railway verge area yesterday, he knows it wasn't agreed, and he apologized, but it wasn't planned. He heard a noise from under the decking, Spud continued, and assuming it was the UDFF, went to give them what for. He could smell them, and during the pursuit, he leapt over the decking fence at the North East end of the garden area and found himself in the railway verge area chasing the UDFF East towards up Town. Spud added that by the time he got to the busted sofa area, he had lost all scent of them.
    5.3 Spencer: Spencer stated that that was a mad thing to do, and presumably the busted sofa area was all clear. It was, replied Spud, no sign of anything, so he had a wee rest and then decided that as he was so close, he would go on for a few more klicks to The Farm, and have a good butchers. Did you

see Karen the Sheep? asked Spencer. He did, replied Spud; she looked her usual miserable self. Well at least we know she's still alive and not a pre-packed lamb dhansak, said Ada.

5.4 Horny Frank: Horny Frank stated that it's very concerning that the UDFF are still at it, and that should be discussed at the Council of Five meeting today as well. This is still a long tail issue, continued Horny Frank, just because they call themselves a break-away group means nothing, and Ben the Long Tail needs to understand that. Horny Frank added that Princess Snickerdoodle should clamp down on this type of activity, even if she has to take draconian measures to do so. What's draconian measures? asked Spud. No idea replied Horny Frank, but he knows that it's very effective for those who don't toe the line. We can't have long tails wandering around willy nilly and unrestricted, there's far too many of them now having these new enhanced freedom ideas, it has to be nipped in the bud, stated Horny Frank. We have to be very careful here, argued Beardy, we can't just stop the long tails having their own wee thoughts, they have a right to those wee thoughts. Yes, but as long it doesn't interfere with our wee thoughts, thoughts can't be all mixed up like that, it's not right, replied Horny Frank.

5.5 Ada: Ada stated that she's all up for draconian measures, they sound great, and it should be definitely tabled today at the Council of Five meeting. Princess Snickerdoodle needs to start restricting her long tails for sure, she should only let some out at certain times, and any other long tails out and about are presumed to be up to no good and should be detained and their kin isolated, and maybe dish out a bit of what for just for good measure. Spud stated that he agreed with Ada and will definitely be making those suggestions today. Spud also stated that he would be having a pre-meet with Lulu to let her know what the Board's narrative will be during the Council of Five meeting. Where will this meeting take place? asked the Chair, he doesn't want to be eyeballing this tryst during his crispy dry time! Good point, said Ada, especially the future meetings when there's a hard Border at the 209 Meridian. The plan is, replied Spud, to have the meeting at the fence on the Board's garden area on the far North West side, just before the perimeter area, and next to Her Nextdoor's cabbage patch, well out of the Chair's crispy dry eyeballing range. Ada has a tunnel there for access between the two garden areas, continued Spud, so Gregory the Pecker can enter Her

Nextdoor's cabbage patch from the railway verge area West of the 209 Meridian, Lulu should already be there, Foxy and the foxy nosed Fox and Ben the Long Tail can enter the Board's garden area via the railway verge area East of 209 Meridian. Sweet as replied Ada.
6. Other business – None

49. SPECIAL UNIT FOR FOREIGN AFFAIRS

49th Lockdown Board Meeting: Fri, 8th May 2020

In Attendance:

Me (Chair)

Spud II (Head of cat dept)

Spencer (Head of bigger dog dept)

Ada (Head of smaller dog dept)

Horny Frank (Head of horny rabbit dept)

Beardy (Head of not so horny rabbit dept)

Apologies - None

Call to order 06:00hrs

1. There were sufficient members for a quorum
2. Minutes of previous meeting approved
3. Business from last meeting: None
4. Statement from the Chair: Boris stated yesterday that lockdown easing won't be a quickie, but the weekend will be a lovely crispy dry one, so that's good. Boris also received an open letter from top Industry CEOs from Ben and Jerry's, Iceland Foods and Barrett Homes, stating that when Boris starts repairing the damaged economy, he must not include polluting industries, so that's interesting. PPE from Turkey was a bit dodgy, so that's not good.
5. Business Updates:
    5.1 Spud: Spud stated that the first Council of Five meeting went very well. Main objectives were agreed, and they are as follows:
      5.1.1 Projects of mass beautification are to be monitored closely.
      5.1.2 Special attention to be given to relationships between long tail break-away groups, Regan's Special Branch and the up Town Mob.
      5.1.3 The Council of Five will have legitimate powers to form a military coalition, to search for, capture or drive out alien visitor types in the railway verge area between Elsewhere and up Town, regardless of the 209 Meridian Border.
      5.1.4 The Board's Special Operations Unit will be upregulated to form the new military coalition, which will involve foreign internal defence, psychological operations, and theatre search and rescue. The Unit will be renamed, the Special Unit for Foreign Affairs.
      5.1.5 The long tails insisted on having a Flag to represent the new Council, so designs were put forward quickly and Spud and Lulu's design got the most votes, it'll be published with these minutes.
    5.2 Horny Frank: Horny Frank stated that it all sounds very imposing, but what does it mean? It means that our first main actions are to get Karen the Sheep back in safe paws, replied Spud, and to understand Elsewhere and the West area better, and help the peckers with their local issues, for example, the horned coot attacks on the pecker kids and missus Pecker's wee eggs.

5.3 Spencer: Spencer congratulated Spud on his first meeting as a diplomatic official. Spencer asked who will be involved in the new Special Ops Unit and can they call it the 'SUFA' for short. Call it whatever you want, replied Spud, but it was agreed that the frontline operatives would be Lulu and Ben the Long Tail with Ada in charge, and the back office would be Gregory the Pecker covering the West, and Foxy the foxy nosed Fox covering the East with Spud overseeing both. Well played, Spud replied Spencer, very neatly done indeed. Well, added Spud, he did get a lot of support from Lulu, which was planned of course. So, the Board is pretty much in the driver's seat, stated Spencer. Pretty much replied Spud, but it does mean we have to be on our toes at all times. We are going to need a few quick wins very soon, stated Spencer, to prove to our Stakeholders that this is all worth the effort. There's a lot of speculation surrounding Karen the Sheep at the moment, so some movement toward resolving that issue would be good for the optics Spencer stated.

5.4 Beardy: Beardy asked, that how come he and Horny Frank didn't have a new role to play? You already play a big role, argued Spud, you two and Spencer are very much our Home Guard. Ada added that Horny Frank's code name could be Private Godfrey. That's rich coming from Harold Steptoe, argued Horny Frank! All joking aside, said Spencer, Spud is right, we need to keep our backend covered at all times.

5.5 Ada: Before Ada started her update, the Chair interrupted and asked Ada where all the pigeon feathers came from yesterday? A pigeon, replied Ada, she was going to discuss the incident during her update if given half a chance! It had nothing to do with her, added Ada, it all happened while the Chair was sound asleep around 13:00hrs during his crispy dry time. The Chair stated that he was only having a wee snoozette in the hot midday sun, and then he awoke to find the garden area covered in feathers, with Ada right smack bang in the middle of it all! Well, Ada replied, when you were in the middle of your wee snoozette, a pigeon type paid us an unsolicited visit. The cheek of it too interrupted Spud; he was having a wee early afternoon snoozette too in his favourite spot, just before he had to attend the Council of Five meeting, when as bold as you like, this pigeon type landed two feet from him. So, of course the pigeon type had to be given what for, and off he flew with a serious haircut. Shouldn't we have detained the pigeon type asked Horny Frank, instead of letting him go like?

No point argued Spud, the pigeon types are as thick as. That's all well and good, explained the Chair, but there's still the issue of all the feathers! Spud and Ada won't get the ear-bashing from Her Indoors. When Her Indoors comes home later this evening from a hard day's work, and danders into the garden area with her latte in hand and sits down at the crispy dry table for a relaxed natter with the Chair, she won't see a lovely sunset and a somewhat sun-kissed twinkled eyed Irishman, who's fond of relaxing with the odd crispy dry one, oh no, what she'll see is the garden area covered in pigeon feathers and baked guff, and an aberration of a burnt-faced languorous pisshead. All because Spud gave a pigeon what for, added the Chair. Butterfly effect said Beardy.

6. Other business – The Chair stated that the Stakeholders want a map of the area which the Chair will commission and keep the Board updated on its progress.

50. THE BACKSLIDER

50th Lockdown Board Meeting: Sat, 9th May 2020

In Attendance:

Me (Chair)

Spud II (Head of cat dept)

Spencer (Head of bigger dog dept)

Ada (Head of smaller dog dept)

Horny Frank (Head of horny rabbit dept)

Beardy (Head of not so horny rabbit dept)

Apologies - None

Call to order 06:00hrs

1. There were sufficient members for a quorum
2. Minutes of previous meeting approved

3. Business from last meeting: The Chair stated that the drawing of a map has been commissioned and should be completed and published tomorrow.
4. End of the Week Statement from the Chair: We have been in lockdown now for seven weeks! I want to thank all departments for their cooperation during these stressful times. Our lovable Stakeholders are all still losing the plot, we have 282 of them now in our wee community which is mad, and they're still happy to continue to read the ramblings of a complete headcase, they know not what they do. So, we will go on for a bit longer. The Lockdown continues but slightly easing now. This is our 50th daily meeting and 100 days since the very first infection here!
5. Statement from the Chair: The TUC's Ms O'Grady stated that parents and school staff need full confidence before schools are to reopen, so that's good. The NAHT and the NEU have called for clear, scientific published evidence, that schools will be safe, so that's good too. Banksy drew a picture at Southampton General Hospital, so that's nice.
6. Business Updates:
    6.1 Ada: Ada stated that the Special Unit for Foreign Affairs agreed on a reconnaissance mission to The Farm, and yesterday afternoon at 13:00hrs, Ben the Long Tail and herself headed out. There was no sign of border patrols at the 209 Meridian, so they headed East through the thickety thickets. Unfortunately, the recon mission was cut short because of a very heavy Special Branch presence at the busted sofa area. They counted at least ten agents, pretty much ready for business. They observed the Special Branch from a safe distance and then headed back through the thickety thickets.
    6.2 Spud: Spud stated that that was odd, the last couple of days the busted sofa area was all clear, not a sinner to be seen, and now it's crawling with Special Branch agents. It's almost as if they know we've upped our game. Ada stated that that concerns her, if Regan from the Special Branch knows about the Council of Five or the formation of the Special Unit for Foreign Affairs, then how did he get that information? That didn't take long, interrupted Spencer, potential backslider in our midst. That's all we need at the moment, added Ada.
    6.3 Spencer: Spencer stated that when life gives you lemons, juggle them. Go ahead with the next mission, nothing too exciting, and let's see what happens, added Spencer. Definitely replied Spud, today Ada should head West for a rendezvous with Gregory the Pecker at the incredible machine, and the

brief should only be to discuss coot activity in the local vicinity, nothing more than that until you get there, that should keep things tight. Ada agreed and stated that she'd take Ben the Long Tail again, as Lulu and Foxy the foxy nosed Fox are busy with other stuff.

6.4 Horny Frank: Horny Frank stated that when life gives you lemons, you should do the lemon dance to the lemon song. Thank you for your very wise advice, replied Ada, very helpful it was too. Just trying to lighten the mood, said Horny Frank, no need to get all peevish. Ada stated that she's not being peevish, she's just trying to think. If we have a backslicer in our midst, added Ada, that's a very big problem, juggling a few lemons is one thing but doing a dance is a different thing altogether. You do realise that the lemon thing is just a figure of speech? argued Horny Frank. Really, replied Ada, she did not know that and thanked Horny Frank for his lesson on metaphysics. That still sounds a bit peevishy, replied Horny Frank.

6.5 Beardy: Beardy stated that the Chair was a busy boy yesterday, did he receive the ear-bashing he was looking forward to? Well, stated the Chair, no ear-bashing was dished out, because Her Indoors came home late on Thursday night, so never noticed the pigeon feathers in the garden area and she was up and out early yesterday morning so quickly, she again never saw the mess, so big result. But then, added the Chair, the bombshell hit! Her Indoors only went and left a note! The note stated that she'd be home by lunchtime!! So, continued the Chair, after yesterday's meeting he decided to clear away the pigeon feathers, he did a serious baked guff-run, did the food-run and then cut the grass for good measure. It did, however, eat into his crispy dry afternoon somewhat, by then it was 11:15hrs, 45 minutes late! He had no sooner finished his first crispy dry one, and poised to pour the second, the Chair continued, when Her Indoors appeared in the garden area. Now, he didn't expect praise for the cleaning up of the pigeon feathers, as they in theory never existed, nor did he expect serious laudation for the large baked guff collection, as the guff shouldn't have been there in the first place. But maybe, just maybe some sort of positive reinforcement regarding the cutting of the grass, just a wee nod of appreciation would have sufficed. What actually happened was, added the Chair, she arrived by the crispy table and looked over the garden area, the Chair gave her a fizzy one, which she took and sipped without shifting her gaze. Then her first words were uttered, 'you cut the grass!' 'I was going to do that today, and you've left bits out too,' so she went and cut the grass again! Still, stated Beardy, no ear-bashing. Very true, replied the Chair, and it was a lovely hot afternoon, and the crispy dry flowed. Sounds like the making of a new song added Beardy.

7. Other business – None

51 ADA GOES MISSING

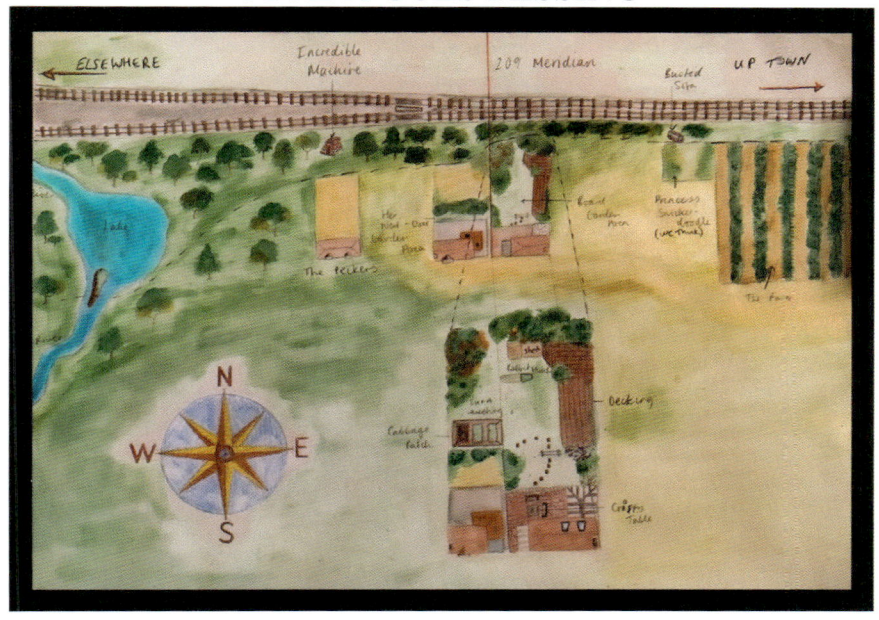

51st Lockdown Board Meeting: Sun, 10th May 2020

In Attendance:

Me (Chair)

Spud II (Head of cat dept)

Spencer (Head of bigger dog dept)

Horny Frank (Head of horny rabbit dept)

Beardy (Head of not so horny rabbit dept)

Apologies - None

Call to order 06:15hrs

1. There were sufficient members for a quorum
2. Minutes of previous meeting approved
3. Business from last meeting: The Chair stated that the drawing of a map has been completed and is published with these minutes. The

scale is not accurate of course but should hopefully give our incredible Stakeholders a better idea of the area. Any questions at all, post them in the our wee community group: https://www.facebook.com/groups/680667366014480/?ref=bookmarks

4. Statement from the Chair: Boris will make last Thursday's announcement later today, regarding easing the Lockdown, so that's late. The Government will launch the new - Alert System in England, so that's interesting. Boris now tells the public to - Stay Alert and Save Lives, so that's interesting too.
5. Business Updates:
    5.1 Ada: Ada did not attend, and there were no apologies received.
    5.2 Spencer: Spencer stated that he apologises for the late start this morning. Unfortunately, Ada had not returned home from her missions yesterday. She left here at 11:00hrs yesterday just after the food-run and met up with Ben the Long Tail at the 209 Meridian. Spencer also stated that he eyeballed this meet-up at the 209 Meridian, and at that point, all was well. The 209 Meridian Border was not patrolled, and he watched them head off West in the Elsewhere direction.
    5.3 Beardy: Beardy stated that he had a visit from the long tails last night too. Ben the Long Tail never returned back either. They were very agitated, not sure that they entirely believed Beardy. Beardy told them that the Board ran search parties earlier with no luck, unfortunately, and will renew the search again first thing at daybreak. The long tails stated that they are going to inform Princess Snickerdoodle about the incident and get back to us.
    5.4 Spud: Spud stated that Ada and Ben the Long Tail headed out on a Special Unit for Foreign Affairs mission to the West, and their first point of call was at the peckers. They were to meet up with Gregory the Pecker at the incredible machine and at that point Ada was to discuss the *actual* mission plan. Up until that point, only Spud and Ada knew what the plan actually was; they thought it was safer keeping it tight that way. The plan wasn't just to rendezvous with Gregory the Pecker and discussed local coot activity; it was to proceed to the outskirts of Elsewhere itself and have a good butchers. Yesterday evening at 19:00hrs, knowing that Ada hadn't returned, Spud stated that he headed out to the peckers to discuss the Board's concerns regarding Ada being missing. He met Gregory the Pecker at the incredible machine, and Gregory the Pecker

stated that Ada, Ben the Long Tail and himself did, in fact meet up yesterday. They discussed the recent horned coot attacks, they agreed on potential defence scenarios and planned to put them to the test very soon. Gregory the Pecker stated that Peckerhead and the rest of the peckers were extremely happy about that. Then Gregory the Pecker added that Ada stated that they were going to continue to Elsewhere! Gregory the Pecker stated that he was somewhat concerned about such a mission because it's unknown territory, and Ben the Long Tail wasn't too happy about it either. However, continued Gregory the Pecker, Ada was unperturbed, and they headed further West on towards Elsewhere, and that was the last time Gregory the Pecker had seen them. They were to stop by on their way back for to update him, Gregory the Pecker added, but they were a no show!

5.5 Horny Frank: Horny Frank stated that that's very bad, we were looking good there for a moment, now it feels like the noose is tightening. No need to panic just yet, replied Spencer, remember this is Ada we are talking about, for all we know she's found a big pile of rubbish, and she thinks it's Christmas. But it's Ben the Long Tail too, argued Horny Frank, the fact that both of them are missing suggests something quite different. Let's just stay calm, Spencer reiterated, he and Spud will head out into the railway verge area again this morning for another search as agreed. Definitely, stated Spud, Gregory the Pecker has also agreed to help, so let's not jump to any conclusions just yet. Spencer asked Spud if there were any further communications with the long tails yet? Spud replied that he hadn't heard a thing from the long tails.

6. Other business – None

52. A NEW STICK

52nd Lockdown Board Meeting: Mon, 11th May 2020

In Attendance:

Me (Chair)

Spud II (Head of cat dept)

Spencer (Head of bigger dog dept)

Horny Frank (Head of horny rabbit dept)

Beardy (Head of not so horny rabbit dept)

Apologies - None

Call to order 06:15hrs

1. There were sufficient members for a quorum
2. Minutes of previous meeting approved

3. Business from last meeting: None
4. Statement from the Chair: Boris stated yesterday that falling down the stairs is the worst bit, so that's good. Boris also stated that primary schools would open on the 1st June, and two people from two different households can meet and sunbath in the park, so that's good too. The Government has missed it's 100,000 daily tests target eight days in a row, so that's interesting.
5. Business Updates:
    5.1 Ada: Ada did not attend, and there were no apologies received.
    5.2 Spud: Spud stated that Ada and Ben the Long Tail have still not returned home from their mission out West on Saturday. After the food-run yesterday Spud continued, and just as crispy dry time was beginning, he crossed over the perimeter area between the railway verge area and the garden area into the railway verge area and headed West. Once again, the 209 Meridian Border was not manned. By the time he reached the peckers, Gregory the Pecker and Peckerhead were waiting for him at the incredible machine. Peckerhead stated that although he's not a member of the Council or Special Units, he would still like to tag along and help. He was extremely grateful to the Board for rescuing the pecker kids the Peckerhead added, so he must help Spud get Ada back home safe.
    5.3 Spencer: Spencer stated that that was pretty decent of the peckers. Bet the clucking was somewhat irksome though, added Spencer? You're not joking, replied Spud, every five minutes they would just wander around in circles clucking away to themselves, it's like pecker Tourettes. Nonetheless, added Spud, he was glad of their help. So the pace was a bit slow then? asked Spencer. It sure was, replied Spud, but we eventually got to the area Spencer called the enchantment of nature. Wonderful wasn't it? interrupted Spencer. It was very different to the thickety thickets we're used to, replied Spud, and it definitely gave the peckers more room to cluck about. When they eventually finished their clucking through the feathered grasses, we decided to split up and search.
    5.4 Horny Frank: Horny Frank stated that he couldn't believe this is all happening, poor wee Ada. She's probably being held prisoner somewhere, and regularly given what for just for good measure! Well, we don't know that, replied Spencer, his money is still on Ada taking off on one of her detours and maybe getting lost, but she has a great nose on her, and she'll

find her way back. Absolutely, agreed Spud, and think of the stories she'll have to tell, all the amazing bits of rubbish she found. Horny Frank asked if the search of paradise gave up any clues? Not really, replied Spud, he could tell Ada was there, he could still smell her and oddly enough could smell Ben the Long Tail too! Usually there's so much long tail stink closer to home it's a complete Jacobson overload, but here in paradise there's much less long tail stink, which is excellent, and he could just make out Ben the Long Tail's wee stinky stink. That suggests there were not too many long tails around! said Spencer. Sure does replied Spud, which was very interesting in itself, but there were a few different smells there also, and they were very close by.

5.5 Beardy: Beardy stated that it must be nice living somewhere where there aren't many long tails around. Horny frank stated that he didn't mind the long tails at all, at least you know where you stand with them, now the foxy nosed foxes are a very questionable creature type all together if we're looking for a backslider, Horny Frank added, we should start looking there first! Anyway, Spud interrupted, Gregory the Pecker stated that he could see a waterway far in the distance with his farsighted eye but couldn't proceed any further as it was getting late and Peckerhead was getting tired. So that's very interesting, stated Horny Frank, Gregory the Pecker has a farsighted eye! It's not really that interesting, replied Spud, all peckers have a farsighted and a short-sighted eye, but it's the waterway bit that's interesting. Another thing that's very interesting, Spud continued, along with the new stinks that he couldn't quite place, they were also being watched from the very moment they entered paradise, he could just feel their sneaky wee eyes on the back of his neck. That's all well and good, but that's another day gone, stated Beardy, maybe we need a bigger search party? The long tails have gone very quiet, no foxy nosed foxes offering to help, and Lulu is nowhere to be seen added Beardy. Well replied Spud, the long tails are probably pursuing their own search and rescue, just like we are, and that's ok for the moment. Lulu is busy in up Town and probably doesn't know yet, and he has no idea what the foxy nosed foxes are up to. So, interrupted Spencer, same again today then? Absolutely, agreed Spud, he's all ready to go right after this meeting, and he's going alone this time, no more clucking from the clucking peckers, he's heading

straight for the waterway in paradise, he's sure the clues are there.
6. Other business – None

53. SANDY CHEEKS

53rd Lockdown Board Meeting: Tues, 12th May 2020

In Attendance:

Me (Chair)

Spud II (Head of cat dept)

Spencer (Head of bigger dog dept)

Ada (Head of smaller dog dept)

Horny Frank (Head of horny rabbit dept)

Beardy (Head of not so horny rabbit dept)

Apologies - None

Call to order 06:15hrs

1. There were sufficient members for a quorum
2. Minutes of previous meeting approved
3. Business from last meeting: None
4. Statement from the Chair: Boris's mate Rishi stated that he has to pay six million people 80% of their wages, so that's not good. Boris added that it's, one of the most remarkable features of the Government's response, so that's good. Richard Branson stated that he was financially struggling and will have to sell something, maybe his space tourism business, so that's good too.
5. Business Updates:
    5.1 Spud: Spud stated he was delighted to see Ada back home safe again. Spud said that on his second mission back West yesterday, he finally tracked Ada down, and as it happened, she was on her way back home anyway. Ada stated that she really does apologize for worrying everybody, unfortunately it couldn't be helped, as circumstances dictated an unplanned change to their mission. What about Ben the Long Tail? asked Spencer. Well, we parted company replied Ada, not long before she met up with Spud, but she'll explain that in her update.
    5.2 Horny Frank: Horny Frank stated that he was thinking the worst and was really pleased she's home safe and sound. Horny Frank added that he knew there was something problematic with that Ben the Long Tail, or any long tail for that matter. Well to be fair to Ben the Long Tail, replied Ada, he didn't know we were heading for Elsewhere, so what happened wasn't really his fault. Horny Frank added that he's sure Ben the Long Tail didn't help the situation either!
    5.3 Ada: Ada stated that she would walk them through the chain of events. After leaving the peckers on Saturday, and dropping the bombshell about going further West to Elsewhere, Ben the Long Tail was not a happy chappy, in fact, he was getting very ratty. Gregory the Pecker had warned us about continuing West, as nobody really knows what's out that way, and Ben the Long Tail just wouldn't let it go, Ada added, so she ripped his head off! Nah - she was only joking, but she felt like it! Anyway, she continued, after about a klick further we came to the thinning of the thickety thickets and arrived at Spencer's Paradise place.
    5.4 Spencer: Spencer stated that it's such a beautiful place and that he so can't wait to go back there again. It was pleasant

enough, replied Ada, a bit too pretty for her liking, she likes a few stingy nettles here and there, with the odd strategically placed mountain of goodies, Paradise is for when you're dead, and you're dead a long time. Anyway, Ada continued, we didn't dither any, we continued to head West toward Elsewhere as planned, and Ben the Long Tail was getting less ratty and started to talk about his family. At first, Ada stated that she couldn't help but think as Ben the Long Tail harped on about his family, that this was so san fairy ann until he mentioned his wife. Well shizzle yur tizzle and fizzle me pizzle, his wife is only his mother, and she's just dropped twelve long tail kids! Ben the Long Tail has twelve kids to his mother? You couldn't write this stuff, replied Spencer.

5.5 Beardy: Beardy stated that it's no wonder they look the way they do, bet you they're great banjo players too. Beardy added that he always thought Horny Frank was a bit different, but Ben the Long Tail is right up there with the best. That's not the funny bit, interrupted Ada, the mother's name is Madonna, when he told her that, added Ada, she leaked out of every orifice! Anyway, continued Ada, she could feel herself starting to leak again, so back to the main feature. After a further couple of klicks West, we came across a lake which was somewhat unexpected. On top of that, it was getting late. We agreed that it was too late to head back, and we would have to camp down for the night. There wasn't much to see, only one house across the lake, but we had no idea how to get to it. As we were debating sleeping arrangements, continued Ada, we had a couple of visitors, made her jump, but not as high as Ben the Long Tail, he made Horny Frank look like an amateur. Anyway, these visitor types flew down from the trees like some type of ninja attack, and they looked like the offspring of Horny Frank and Ben the Long Tail's mother, with wings! One of them approached us and said that his name was Sandy Cheeks, and asked what our intentions were. Ada stated that they came from way back East and were lost, and getting ready to camp down for the night. Well East is that way Sandy Cheeks replied, pointing Eastward, make sure you head that way in the morning. And then stated Ada, as quick as you like they foxtrot oscared back up into the trees from whence they came. Took us a while to sleep after that, and the night was getting cold, so she had to spoon Ben the Long Tail, who really didn't produce any heat at all or mould up well, not like Spencer. However, the next morning, Ada continued, Ben the Long Tail had disappeared, she couldn't even get a whiff of his stink anywhere, except on herself! She searched the lake's edge in both directions and found nothing, not even a way across the lake, next thing she knew it was getting dark again! By that time Ada continued, she was heading back Eastward and reached Paradise again, but by then it was dark, and she decided to camp down for the night once more, and that night was even colder, and she had to snuggle up to a shaggy soldier. The next morning very surprisingly, she was awakened by Ben the Long Tail, and she asked where he'd been all this time! He stated that he'd been walking all night, and just wanted to get back home and that they'd catch up later, and then he legged it! That's it really, added Ada, she got her act together and was heading for home, when she bumped into Spud coming in the opposite direction.

6. Other business – None

54. ROBINS CIDER

54th Lockdown Board Meeting: Wed, 13th May 2020

In Attendance:

Me (Chair)

Spud II (Head of cat dept)

Spencer (Head of bigger dog dept)

Ada (Head of smaller dog dept)

Horny Frank (Head of horny rabbit dept)

Beardy (Head of not so horny rabbit dept)

Apologies - None

Call to order 06:15hrs

1. There were sufficient members for a quorum
2. Minutes of previous meeting approved
3. Business from last meeting: None
4. Statement from the Chair: Boris's mate Matt stated yesterday that golf clubs and estate agents could reopen, so that good, but playgrounds can't, so that's not so good. Some people can also go

back to work today, so that's interesting. Boris's mate Mr Jenrick stated that he wants to make life healthy and bearable, while saving lives, so that's nice.

5. Business Updates:
   5.1 Spud: Spud stated that after the Lockdown Board Meeting yesterday which included Ada's disappearance update, he decided to call an urgent Council of Five meeting. Word was sent out to the members, and the meeting took place near Her Nextdoor's Cabbage Patch again, at 14:30hrs, just as the Chair was nodding off after his crispy dry time. Gregory the Pecker, Ben the Long Tail, Foxy the foxy nosed Fox and Spud were in attendance, Lulu couldn't make it down from up Town, but should be back down soon. Foxy the foxy nosed Fox knew nothing about what was going on over this last couple of days. He stated that he was glad Ada was back home safe but was very concerned that all this had happened, and he had heard nothing from the Board nor from the Snickerdoodles, all information was suppressed. How can we trust each other when we don't trust each other? asked Ben the Long Tail.
   5.2 Beardy: Beardy stated that that was rich coming from a foxy nosed fox type. Surely, they have their own Intelligence agency, and surely, they would've heard something on the grid about the issue! He doesn't believe for one moment they didn't know anything about Ada and Ben the Long Tail's disappearance, Beardy added. Well replied Spud; it's very early days for all this trust stuff to come into effect, we are all still playing our cards close to our chests. Yet, added Beardy, it's hardly cricket now, is it!
   5.3 Horny Frank: Horny Frank stated that he agreed with Beardy, there's no way the foxy nosed foxes didn't know anything, all our Stakeholders knew about it, and they can't hold their own water! Anyway, continued Spud, he asked Ben the Long Tail to update us on the events that led to his disappearance from his point of view. Ben the Long Tail confirmed everything Ada told us yesterday, right up until she fell asleep. Ada had been asleep for a while, Ben the Long Tail said, but he was having some trouble sleeping, thinking about those flying ninja type things, and the fact that he and Ada were so far away from home. Plus, Ada had him in such a serious spoon and was making funny noises and licking his ear, like she was having some type of spasm-like tic. Then she'd let out these loud fluffer-doodles, and they stank, it bought water to his

eyes with the irritation from the tiny molecules of kak speck, whatever she's eating, she has to change it.

5.4 Ada: Ada stated that she was somewhat affronted, she likes to think of herself as a private tooter, of course sometimes there's a bit of a lump in it, but still it never stinks- well not to the level of it disturbing a long tail! The point Ben the Long Tail was trying to make, replied Spud, is that he was awake, and you were asleep. So, continued Spud, Ben the Long Tail said that he eventually removed himself from Ada's spoon, and had a walk down to the edge of the lake. The lake was peaceful with its shimmering emptiness, monastically quiet with a whiff of mint, which was a pleasant change from Ada's bum grenades when out of the blue he saw a robin redbreast. He remembers thinking that this was a bit weird at the time, the robin said hi, and stated that his name was Rob. Fair enough, Ben the Long Tail thought, then before he could say ouch ouch ouch, a group of flying ninja type things were on top of him giving him a serious what for! During the fracas, he felt himself being dragged along the ground for a while, and then ended up inside a tree of all places!

5.5 Spencer: Spencer stated that those flying ninja things sound like a serious squad, especially if they hide inside trees, in an area full of trees! Was Ben the Long Tail badly hurt? asked Spencer, and what did they want? Well, said Spud, Ben the Long Tail stated that he was ok, and tried to give them what for back but there were far too many of them, plus that Rob the Robin was there too, with another robin that Robin called Rusty. That's very interesting, said Spencer, robins in bed with these flying ninja type things. The flying ninja type thing they met earlier called Sandy Cheeks, turned up, and asked the same questions over and over again regarding Ada and Ben the Long Tail's intentions. However, the strange thing was, they all seemed to be a bit pished! Nothing odd about that at all, it was probably their crispy dry time, and you interrupted it, interrupted the Chair. Well, it is a bit odd argued Spud, especially when Ben the Long Tail stated that it's the robins that make the pish juice. They even offered Ben the Long Tail some. Did he have some? asked Spencer. Yes, apparently he did, replied Spud. So, Ben the Long Tail had a crispy dry one, laughed Spencer. Well, he said it tasted more like rotten apples covered in vinegar. Cider interrupted the Chair again, Her Indoors does like the odd drop of homemade cider, if you go back, pick some up. So, said Horny Frank, are we really saying that there's a round of robins brewing and pushing cider out West? Correct, replied Spud. Is there no end to this sheer madness? asked Horny Frank. Apparently not replied Spud.

6. Other business – None

55. SPUD'S EYEBALLING EVENT

55th Lockdown Board Meeting: Thurs, 14th May 2020

In Attendance:

Me (Chair)

Spud II (Head of cat dept)

Spencer (Head of bigger dog dept)

Ada (Head of smaller dog dept)

Horny Frank (Head of horny rabbit dept)

Beardy (Head of not so horny rabbit dept)

Apologies - None

Call to order 06:15hrs

1. There were sufficient members for a quorum
2. Minutes of previous meeting approved
3. Business from last meeting: None
4. Statement from the Chair: NHS bosses are urging patients with other medical problems such as cancer and heart concerns, to seek medical treatment if needed, so that's important. NHS England has stated that A&E attendances have dropped dramatically since the pandemic started, so that's not good. Boris's mate Dr Harries stated yesterday that different households could now meet in bubbles, so that's good.
5. Business Updates:
    5.1 Spud: Spud stated that he had a very weird incident yesterday evening. Spencer and Ada were in the kitchen area having a snoozette, and he was just heading out into the garden area for a piddle. When no sooner had he finished, he came face to face with a foxy nosed fox. Spud stated that he didn't recognise him at all, and they stood there just eyeballing each other for a few minutes. The foxy nosed fox was of reasonable size, but Spud said he was sure he could give it what for if it tried anything.
    5.2 Horny Frank: Horny Frank stated that he witnessed the whole eyeballing event. He was catching forty himself when he got a sniff of it. When he had a butchers, he saw Spud and the foxy nosed fox just five feet apart ready to give each other what for. The foxy nosed fox was never giving him what for, argued Spud, he was just waiting on him making the first move, so he could tear him a new one and call it self-defence. The fact that he's in the garden area without invitation is defensible enough, stated Horny Frank. Spud stated that he appreciated that at the time, but these are very delicate times at the moment, and he knew he'd have to face Foxy the foxy nosed Fox in the Council of Five, so he wanted to make sure there was no come back whatsoever.
    5.3 Beardy: Beardy stated that he never saw a thing, he was inside the hutch having his snoozette too, you must've nearly wet yourself! Not at all, replied Spud, he just had a piddle and was all ready to go, his sympathetics were on overdrive. So what happened then? asked Beardy. Well just before it came to blows, Her Indoors walked outdoors into the garden area, lifted a brush and chucked it at the foxy nosed fox and it legged it. Back of the net, replied Beardy. Well, a bit of a

spoiler if he was to be honest, said Spud, he was looking forward to giving that foxy nosed Fox a serious what for. Anyway, added Spud, Her Indoors thought he was in shock and picked him up and give him a good cuddle, but he reckons that Her Indoors was somewhat shocked and needed the cuddle herself, so he went along with it.

5.4 Ada: Ada stated that she was sorry about that, she was indeed having a wee snoozette with Spencer when she caught the tail end of the shenanigans, by the time she shot out through the cat flap and into the garden area, the cuddling phase had begun. Like he said, said Spud, it was no train crash, all was in hand. Fair enough, replied Ada, but we need to have a serious word with Foxy the foxy nosed Fox very soon for an explanation. Definitely, said Spud, he'll track him down later. The Chair stated that he got an ear-bashing about the whole debacle, and added that the whole idea of having these groups and meetings was to keep the garden area tight during these stressful times, how can it be tight when visitor types dander in and out the garden area whenever they like, scaring the bejesus out of Her Indoors, and resulting in him getting an ear-bashing? Ada stated that it was very slack of them, it's been a very busy couple of days, and they took their eyes off the ball and was very sorry that it caused grief between the Chair and Her Indoors. To be fair, the Chair added, Her Indoors was ok in the end, he was telling her about the robins making the homemade cider, which she found somewhat amusing, yet intriguing, and he promised that there would be a special mission planned to fetch her some to sample. Spud stated that he would make sure that the request is tabled at the next Council of Five meeting, which happens to be tomorrow. Does Her Indoors like robins cider? asked Ada?

5.5 Spencer: Spencer stated that he too apologises for the current complacency and added that it'll never happen again. We must keep dick all the time now, Spencer added, we will have to stagger our snoozettes. Horny Frank will organise a snoozette rota and manage it from now on, added Spencer. Agreed, replied Horny Frank. Plus, we still have a few outstanding objectives we need to get started on as well, said Spencer. Talking of which, interrupted the Chair, he's been getting lots and lots of flak from our delightful stakeholders. They want this Karen the Sheep issue resolved as soon as, so put that at the top of the agenda. Agreed, stated Spud, it'll be first on the list for tomorrow's Council of Five meeting, and he'll prime

Lulu to make sure we get it actioned immediately. Any further conflabs with Her Nextdoor? asked Spencer. None whatsoever, replied the Chair- why- should there be? No not really replied Spencer, we just need to keep everybody close at the moment, we can't afford any loose ends, maybe Her Nextdoor likes robins cider too? The Chair argued that if Her Indoors catches him even passing a glance at Her Nextdoor, he'll end up with a very loose end indeed!

6.   Other business – None

56. EAST OF THE FARM

56th Lockdown Board Meeting: Fri, 15th May 2020

In Attendance:

Me (Chair)

Spud II (Head of cat dept)

Spencer (Head of bigger dog dept)

Ada (Head of smaller dog dept)

Horny Frank (Head of horny rabbit dept)

Beardy (Head of not so horny rabbit dept)

Apologies - None

Call to order 06:00hrs

1. There were sufficient members for a quorum
2. Minutes of previous meeting approved
3. Business from last meeting: None
4. Statement from the Chair: NHS England has told hospitals to restart routine operations, so that's good. 16 Unions want the NHS to take a 'safety-first' approach as procedures resume, so that's

good too. Unison's Sara Gorton stated yesterday that the safety of patients is paramount, so that's all great.
5. Business Updates:
   5.1 Spud: Spud stated that shortly after yesterday's meeting, he organised a meet-up with Ben the Long Tail to clear up a few things, with regards to today's Council of Five meeting. The meet-up took place at the busted sofa area, once again the area was quiet, not a whiff of any Special Branch nor break-away long tails. The quietness was the first thing Spud mentioned to Ben the Long Tail, and he couldn't understand it either. Spud explained to Ben the Long Tail that the Board is under immense pressure from their Stakeholders to resolve the Karen the Sheep issue as soon as. Ben the Long Tail stated that he couldn't understand why helping Karen the Sheep was so important to the Board, and Spud somewhat agreed but stated that that's politics for you.
   5.2 Beardy: Beardy stated that Spud made the Stakeholders sound like some sort of secret society masterminding all the Boards activities! It's very reasonable to want to help Karen the Sheep, Beardy added, she's been a great help to us, it's not just the Stakeholders who want her back. He doesn't deny that, argued Spud, but the Chair does take a lot of instruction from the Stakeholders, who we know nothing about really, have you ever met one? No, replied Beardy, but to suggest we're being run by Freemason types is a stretch don't you think? Spud argued that he wasn't suggesting that the Chair was involved in the establishment of a new world order or any such thing, but his long dangly bits are nonetheless being tugged at.
   5.3 Horny Frank: Horny Frank stated that he has to agree with Spud on this one. The Chair does take the easy way out all of the time, as long as it doesn't interfere with his crispy dry time. Right calm down, interrupted the Chair, he's hardly a member of the 322 club! He communicates with the Stakeholders regularly to get advice and seek direction, the Chair added, and the Board reports back to the Stakeholders on a daily basis during these stressful times to show that we are managing our time appropriately. So nobody is pulling his long dangly bits, insisted the Chair, just doing his job as the Chair- thank you very much. Her Indoors pulls your strings though doesn't she, sniped Horny Frank. Not true at all argued, the Chair, as long as he completes the 'honeydolist' every day, which is not easy to do before crispy dry time, then all is well with the world. Anyway, Spud interrupted, back to his meet-up with Ben the

Long Tail. Ben the Long Tail agreed to pursue the Karen the Sheep issue and stated that The Farm isn't far from where he and Madonna live, so he'll head to The Farm for a quick butchers, before heading home. Spud stated that he would go with him. They arrived at the North West corner of The Farm shortly after midday, but couldn't see much activity, so they continued further East along The Farm's North end, running parallel with the railway verge area.

5.4 Ada: Ada stated that that's the furthest east we've ever been! Very true, agreed Spud, we went right off the map! The Chair will have to do another map, added Ada. No he won't, replied the Chair. Anyway, said Spud, we were at the North East corner of The Farm and still couldn't see any activity, but we did notice something strange just East of The Farm. Was it up Town? asked Ada. No, but it did look like a weird little village, explained Spud.

5.5 Spencer: Spencer stated that that's all we need, another place full of strange things. The Chair has just completed a map for the Stakeholders, now we're off that map, added Spencer, and Spud thinks the Chair is a Freemason controlled by the illuminati! Spencer stated that he hopes the Chair isn't going to introduce some Dan Brown poppycock into the mix, that would just be full-on Broadmoor! We can't be doing with any of that symbol guff as well, let's not go down that rabbit hole - no offence said Spencer. None taken replied Beardy. My point was, continued Spud, they couldn't see any sheep at The Farm, never mind Karen the Sheep, and yet right next door to The Farm we find these weird-looking buildings, could it be that Karen the Sheep is held up in one of these buildings? That is a possibility, agreed Ada, did you get a closer butchers? No, that was as close as we got. Ben the Long Tail wanted agreement from the Council of Five before going further. Fair enough agreed Ada. So at least the Karen the Sheep issue will be discussed later the day, so that's good.

6. Other Business — None

57. MIKE WITH A Y

57th 'lockdown' Board meeting: Sat, 16th May 2020

In Attendance:

Me (Chair)

Spud II (Head of cat dept)

Spencer (Head of bigger dog dept)

Ada (Head of smaller dog dept)

Horny Frank (Head of horny rabbit dept)

Beardy (Head of not so horny rabbit dept)

Apologies - None

Call to order 06:00hrs

1. There were sufficient members for a quorum
2. Minutes of previous meeting approved
3. Business from last meeting: None
4. End of the Week Statement from the Chair: We have been in lockdown now for eight weeks! I want to thank all departments for their cooperation during these most stressful times. Our lovable

Stakeholders still continue to deal with their cognitive dysfunction. We now have 298 of them in our wee community group, which is still mad. I'd also like to thank all our lovely Stakeholders for their response to the 'continuation poll' during the week; it was very much appreciated. A lot of you have been suggesting that the stories should be put into a book format for a keepsake, which is a great idea and I will endeavour to make that happen. I will discuss ideas and possible next steps in the community group over the next week or so, all ideas welcome and needed, so join us in our mad community group and have your say,
https://www.facebook.com/groups/680667366014480/

5. Statement from the Chair: The Children's Commissioner for England, Anna Longfield, stated that the 'government and teachers should stop squabbling', so that's good. The BMA is backing the teachers' unions stating that infection rates are still too high for schools to reopen, so that's interesting. Police in London has stated that, if you're thinking of having a mass gathering this weekend, don't, so that's interesting too.

6. Business Updates:
   6.1 Spud: Spud stated that Lulu came back down from up Town yesterday and that he gave her a complete update. Unlike Foxy the foxy nosed Fox, Lulu knew all about Ada and Ben the Long Tail's disappearance. The Chair stated that he had a quick conflab with the Girl from up Town when she dropped Lulu off at Her Nextdoor's garden area. He stated that he was in the middle of his honeydolist, and seriously running out of time as the crispy dry time was fast approaching, when there she appeared at the fence area, with some bloke. The Girl from up Town introduced the Chair to her boyfriend, who stated that his name was Mike with a Y.

   6.2 Beardy: Beardy stated that that was a very odd name to have! What else did Mike with a Y have to say for himself? He said he works for some telecoms company up Town. Did Mike with a Y know anything about the beautification project in the railway verge area? asked Beardy. The Chair stated that he never asked him that, why would Beardy assume Mike with a Y knew anything about the beautification project? Well if you remember Karen the Sheep telling us about the poles in the ground, Beardy continued, she said that she thought it was a telecoms company erecting them.

   6.3 Spencer: Spencer stated that it would be hardly fair on Mike with a Y if the Chair started quizzing him on poles in the railway verge area, that Karen the Sheep said fried your brains

and lungs. Exactly, replied Spud, and he's sure Lulu would have informed us if that were the case. Beardy added that he supposed Lulu never mention anything about the poles in the ground at yesterday's Council of Five meeting, did she? No, replied Spud, not a word. However, we did decide at the meeting that the search and rescue mission for Karen the Sheep is a go, and that Ada would take point.

6.4 Ada: Ada stated that she was glad about the decision and is planning to head out right after this meeting, and before the food-run. Ada stated that she is going in heavy with Ben the Long Tail and Foxy the foxy nosed Fox. Their initial plans are to head straight to the weird village just east of The Farm, that's if they don't run into any problems with Regan from the Special Branch or the break-away long tails. Foxy the foxy nosed Fox and Ada will secure the perimeter of the weird village, and Ben the Long Tail will enter the weird-village and have a good butchers at the various dwellings. We will then regroup, analyse the info and make the next decision there and then regarding next steps.

6.5 Horny Frank: Horny Frank stated that that sounds like an excellent plan. What happens if you do rescue Karen the Sheep? asked Horny Frank. Well, replied Ada, we'll just leg it back. 'Leg it back?' repeated Horny Frank, that seems a bit- every creature for himself! It does seem that way, but believe it or believe it not, a lot of preparation went into that decision, replied Ada. All of us have our own way of navigating the railway verge area at high speed, she can manoeuvre low and fast through the thickety thickets, Ben the Long Tail can use the tunnels, Foxy the foxy nosed Fox can use garden areas and jump from bin to bin, and as for Karen the Sheep, well when she gets up a head of steam and charges, there's no stopping her. Actually, insisted Horny Frank, he meant when you all get back to here, what happens to Karen the Sheep? That's a very good point, interrupted the Chair, because she isn't coming into this garden area, there's no way in hell that Her Indoors will play any part in harbouring a stolen sheep, especially during these stressful times! You can hardly call the search and rescue of Karen the Sheep, a 'stolen sheep' situation, argued Horny Frank. He doesn't have to call it anything, replied the Chair, and if Horny Frank has a problem with Her Indoors, he should arrange a meet-up to discuss Her Indoors' bad attitude toward stolen sheep. Ada stated that she would pay good money to watch that meet-up and potential cookery lesson!

Doesn't matter anyway, stated Spud, it was agreed at yesterday's Council of Five meeting, that the peckers garden area would be used as a safe garden for Karen the Sheep, should she be still alive and subsequently freed of course. That makes sense, stated Ada, as it's on the East side of the Border, hopefully, The Farm can't touch her. Exactly replied Spud, the border control might work in our favour this time.

Stakeholders happy, job done, concluded Ada.

7. Other Business – None

58. THE BABY SHEEP

58th Lockdown Board Meeting: Sun, 17th May 2020

In Attendance:

Me (Chair)

Spud II (Head of cat dept)

Spencer (Head of bigger dog dept)

Ada (Head of smaller dog dept)

Horny Frank (Head of horny rabbit dept)

Beardy (Head of not so horny rabbit dept)

Apologies - None

Call to order 06:00hrs

1. There were sufficient members for a quorum
2. Minutes of previous meeting approved
3. Business from last meeting: None
4. Statement from the Chair: Boris has acknowledged frustration, so that's good. Boris stated that £93m would be spent on a 'not-for-

profit' vaccine lab, so that's interesting. Boris's mate Gavin stated that schools must reopen- we owe it to the children, so that's interesting too.

5. Business Updates:
    5.1 Ada: Ada stated that straight after yesterday's meeting, she crossed over the perimeter area between the garden area and the railway verge area and prepared herself to head East toward The Farm. She had planned to meet Foxy the foxy nosed Fox and Ben the Long Tail at the busted sofa as pre-arranged. Before heading off, she noticed that at the border area there were holes dug all the way along the 209 Meridian.
    5.2 Spencer: Spencer stated that that's the beginning of the hard border construct. Spencer added that part of him thought it would never happen, but here it is. Never even heard them dig the holes! Ada stated that she never heard a thing neither. Anyway, Ada continued, apart from the new holes, everything else was pretty much the same. She headed into the thickety thickets which seem to be getting somewhat thicker as the summer approaches and wondered how the workmen physically got to the Border from up Town through all these thickety thickets.
    5.3 Beardy: Beardy stated that they probably got there via the actual railway line area itself. Yes, more than likely agreed Spencer. Ada stated that she must investigate that later, because if workman can access the railway line area, then so can she, which might come in handy at a later date. Beardy stated that he reckons the long tails have tunnels right into the railway line area, and probably over to the other side and beyond. No doubt agreed Ada. Anyway, by the time she reached the busted sofa area, Foxy the foxy nosed Fox and Ben the Long Tail were already there and raring to go.
    5.4 Horny Frank: Horny Frank asked was there any sign of Regan from the Special Branch or the break-away long tails? No, replied Ada, not a squeak. That's very odd too, added Horny Frank, where have they all gone, one minute they were all over the place, now not a squeak! Something is about to happen; she can feel it in her water, stated Ada. So we headed off East towards The Farm, and eventually arrived there just before midday. Once again, The Farm was free of sheep- in fact, free of anything! They continued along the North end of The Farm that runs parallel with the railway verge area, stated Ada until they got to the Northeast corner of The Farm. Ada said that she stopped for a moment and was having a general

butchers, when she noticed in the distance, further East in the railway verge area, one of those long poles Karen the Sheep was telling Beardy about. Beardy stated that he absolutely knew that Karen the Sheep was telling the truth!

5.5 Spud: Spud stated that we weren't debating the existence of the long poles; it was the 'death to us all via laser beams' that we had some scepticism over. You'll wake up soon enough, stated Beardy. Will he indeed, replied Spud. We headed toward the weird village, Ada continued, and as we got there, she and Foxy the foxy nosed Fox took up position at the perimeter area of the weird village to secure it, while Ben the Long Tail prepared himself to enter the weird village. Ada stated that, when all was said and done, she really admired Ben the Long Tail for his bravery, because what he did took some guts. Ada stated that from Ben the Long Tail's account, he entered the weird village area from the West and got closer to the dwellings to get a better butchers. The first dwelling he looked into was empty, but as he approached the second dwelling, he could hear a bleating sound coming from it. When Ben the Long Tail looked inside, he saw a couple of sheep with several baby sheep. It was the same story with the other dwellings too, more sheep and more baby sheep. Then out of the corner of his eye, Ben the Long Tail saw a run-down shack with Karen the Sheep poking her ugly, yet beautiful face out of it. As he got closer, he noticed that Karen the Sheep was tied up, but luckily enough it was just rope, and Ben the Long Tail was able to gnaw his way through it. That was an excellent job well done, stated Spud; you should be really pleased with yourself. Well, replied Ada, like she said, Ben the Long Tail played a blinder, he freed Karen the Sheep from the ropes, and she never saw a sheep run so fast. As Karen the Sheep bulldozed her way through the weird village and out into the railway verge area heading West toward home, continued Ada, that was the cue to begin the 'leg it' phase of the mission, and leg it we did. Is Karen the Sheep safe now? asked Beardy. She sure is, when we eventually caught up with her at the busted sofa area, we explained to her the pecker plan and she was delighted with that, so we headed straight for the peckers garden area and dropped her off safe and sound. Another job well done stated Spencer.

6. Other Business – None

59. THE HARD BORDER GOES UP

59th Lockdown Board Meeting: Mon, 18th May 2020

In Attendance:

Me (Chair)

Spud II (Head of cat dept)

Spencer (Head of bigger dog dept)

Ada (Head of smaller dog dept)

Horny Frank (Head of horny rabbit dept)

Beardy (Head of not so horny rabbit dept)

Apologies - None

Call to order 06:00hrs

1. There were sufficient members for a quorum
2. Minutes of previous meeting approved

3. Business from last meeting: None
4. Statement from the Chair: Security guards are to man train stations now, so that's interesting. Boris's mate Sir Peter stated that - stations are in a better place, and only people who cannot work from home should return to work, so that's good. NHS England launched a, 20-minute on-line training prevention programme to stop people from killing themselves, so that's handy.
5. Business Updates:
    5.1 Beardy: Beardy stated that he had visitors last night. A couple of foxy nosed foxes paid him a visit; they stated that there was a lot of activity in the railway verge area, especially near the border at the 209 Meridian. They said that human types had entered the railway verge area from the railway line area and started to bring stuff in. They also stated that the busted sofa area was heavily manned by Regan from the Special Branch!
    5.2 Horny Frank: Horny Frank stated that there was a lot of noise coming from the railway verge area, kept him awake all night. He got himself all into a right state, continued Horny Frank, he thought they were going to come into the garden area and start dishing out what for! Normally he counts sheep, which helps a lot, but now he just thinks about Karen the Sheep being all tied up in that old run-down shack in that weird village area, like what was that all about, it's almost like they had her there for a particular reason? It's getting really scary now.
    5.3 Spencer: Spencer stated that unfortunately, the day we all dreaded has finally arrived. After his early morning ablutions, he nipped into the railway verge area for a quick butchers, and the People from up Town have only gone and erected a hard border! There is now a hard border between the East and West, a great big metal fence stretching from where our garden perimeter area meets Her Nextdoor's garden perimeter area, right to the railway line area. Very wide and very high, no chance of getting through now.
    5.4 Spud: Spud stated that this was inevitable, we all knew this was coming so there's no need to panic really. Spud stated that he's more concerned about the Special Branch activity now. The hard border goes up, and now Regan from the Special Branch occupies the busted sofa area, that's not a coincidence, they knew that was happening last night and were prepared for any interference. Spud stated that he thinks that the very successful search and rescue mission of Karen the Sheep,

carried out by Ada yesterday, has really spooked them into action.

5.5 Ada: Ada stated that she agrees with Spud, we need to stay focused more than ever now, so they stuck up a metal fence, it's hardly going to stop us from going West now is it. We'll dig a hole under it or access the West part of the railway verge area via Her Nextdoor's garden area. Was there anybody guarding the new hard border? asked Ada. No, replied Spencer, it was all clear. Ada stated that they wouldn't have the humanpower to guard this hard border 24/7, so it's no sweat. Well, that may not be the case, replied Spud, they could use Regan from the Special Branch and his cronies to guard it. We really don't need cronies like Mobbed-up Roger or Tony the Long Tail and their kind hanging around so close outside our garden area added Spud. That's very true agreed Ada, so we need to increase our alert code to amber now. We have to accept the fact that we now have an occupying force in the railway verge area which threatens our freedom; therefore, we must act! We must rise up against these oppressors; they erect hard borders, we will build barricades, Ada added, we will give all that we can give so that our banners may advance, the blood of the martyrs will water the thickety thickets of the railway verge area, do you hear the animals sing! Ok Victor, take a step back, walk away from the barricades, no need to start rioting just yet, insisted Spud, we need to be very smart about what happens next.

6. Other Business – None

60. THE FLAG OF LIBERTY

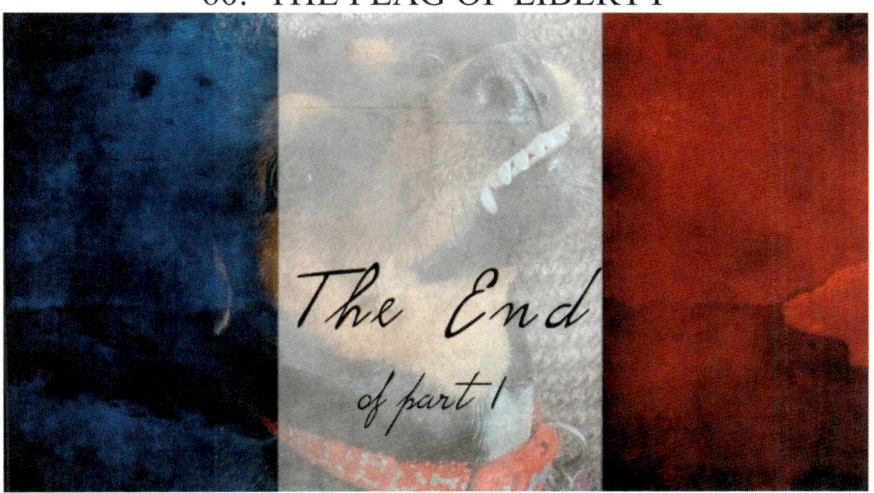

60th Lockdown Board Meeting: Tues, 19th May 2020

In Attendance:

Me (Chair)

Spud II (Head of cat dept)

Spencer (Head of bigger dog dept)

Ada (Head of smaller dog dept)

Horny Frank (Head of horny rabbit dept)

Beardy (Head of not so horny rabbit dept)

Apologies - None

Call to order 06:00hrs

1. There were sufficient members for a quorum
2. Minutes of previous meeting approved
3. Business from last meeting: None
4. End of Story Statement from the Chair: Today marks the 60th day and the 60th story, which now brings it to a natural break in this part of the saga. The 60 stories will be printed into a book format

as requested, which the Chair will action over the few weeks. Hopefully, if all things go to plan, the next part story will continue soon again, as revolution fever builds up. So keep updated on the community group page:
https://www.facebook.com/groups/680667366014480/

5. Statement from the Chair: Boris's mate Matt stated that everyone aged five and over can now be tested, especially if they've lost taste or smell, so that's interesting. NHS providers have stated that test returns could take up to between 5 -13 days, so that's not good. London's Mayor, Mr Khan wants to introduce the new contact tracing regime in the Capital first, so that's interesting. Mr T is actually trying the new drug out himself, the BBC aren't happy about this, and stated that the drug has side-effects, so that's interesting too.

6. Business Updates:

    6.1 Beardy: Beardy asked the Chair what happens next, now that there's no more Lockdown Board Meetings? The Chair stated that we are only taking a wee break for a bit, just to sort out the book malarkey. Ok but what happens to the Board during this time? asked Beardy. Nothing, replied the Chair, you take a wee break from meeting up every morning too, have longer ablutions or maybe have more snoozes.

    6.2 Ada: Ada stated that this natural wee break rest type guff has come at a very inappropriate time. All hell is breaking out in the railway verge area, standards of living are decreasing by the day as the animal populations grow, and the Chair wants to have a wee break! It's only for a short while, and you still have the Council of Five meetings to manage, and a revolution to plan for, so you probably won't even miss the Lockdown Board Meetings, stated the Chair. Ada reiterated that the enlightenment is fast approaching and that no longer will the animals of the railway verge area be dictated to, or brainwashed into catering for the whims of the hidden hands from up Town. You have a wee break, we haven't the time, added Ada.

    6.3 Horny Frank: Horny Frank stated that surely our Stakeholders wouldn't put up with this lackadaisical approach by the Chair, how will they know what our revolutionary plans are? Horny Frank said that he wonders if the Chair is aware of their current situation and is making the right call! Reforms are required for the better treatment of all creature types in the railway verge area, and the Chair is refusing to take responsibility for his part in achieving these reforms. The current practice of reporting to our Stakeholders is our own specially granted freedom, and just when we need to flood them with as much information as we can regarding the so-called beautification project of the railway verge area, you pull the plug. Surely the Board should've voted on this sudden wee rest break guff?

6.4 Spencer: Spencer stated that fortunately it's only a short break and he has absolute confidence in the Chair and his decisions and he's sure the Lockdown Board Meetings will resume as soon as. The Chair thanked Spencer, absolutely correct, if all things go well, we should be up and running again very soon. Exactly, replied Spencer, in the meantime, we have a lot of work to do. Ada was right about the barricade, added Spencer, we need to build one at the perimeter area between the garden area and the railway verge area. Right on it, replied Ada, and we must man the barricade 24/7, so if Horny Frank can do a rota- that would be great. Horny Frank agreed.

6.5 Spud: Spud stated that we don't need a meeting every morning at the moment, let the Chair have his wee rest thingy, we have loads to be getting on with. When the Chair is finished with this book malarkey, he'll be back. He will not be able to ignore us for long; he'll be sitting there having his wee crispy dry moments watching us prepare the barricades and witnessing the birth of the Third Estate, he'll soon be busting his hole to get back in the game. Plus, Spud added, he'll have the Stakeholders constantly on his back, and remember he's their bitch, he'll do what he's told in the end. So let's not wallow in the Chair's 'we need a rest doo-doo', and concentrate more on what we need to be doing for ourselves, and that is to exercise our right to resist oppression from the hidden hand of the People from up Town. Well said agreed Ada, let's build that barricade, plant the flag of liberty right on top of it and prepare to dish out what for to the bitter end.

7. Other Business – None
8. Date of next meeting – TBC

Printed in Great Britain
by Amazon